DEATH
Blinks

New York Times Bestselling Author

TAMARA ROSE BLODGETT

www.tamararoseblodgett.com
TRB Facebook Fan Page: https://www.facebook.com/
AuthorTamaraRoseBlodgett

Editing suggestions provided by Red Adept Editing
Cover art: Willsin Rowe

ISBN-10: 1534849815

ISBN-13: 9781534849815

DEDICATION

Sylvia Mast Bernard

I have not forgotten.

1

Deegan

Fire and ice murder my skin with the pins-and-needles of a numbing sensation as we fall without landing.

My eyes open after being closed so tightly, and the view is dizzying.

The scene is like water skating over glass, where many worlds reveal themselves as though reflected in a room of funhouse mirrors.

Images of many Deegans flash before me as I travel—everything else has slowed to a snail's pace.

Pax *blinked*.

But everyone hitched a ride. The Real Parker—and the Fake Parker.

I cling to Mitchell, the last solid thing from my world, though he belongs to the bot world.

Mitchell is inside my skull. He feels that he belongs to me. But Mitchell is a murderer. And avenging his dead family will not be the last murder he commits.

Happy birthday, Deegan. Today, I turn seventeen, but as I roll into an alternate world, stuff doesn't feel very festive.

In the next moment, we land hard with a sucking pop. Vertigo sinks its wily teeth into my balance—and my brain—as I tumble out of Mitchell's strong embrace.

The world stops spinning, and I slowly take stock of my surroundings.

No one greets me. No family. No crazy-ass Brad Thompson or his corrupt dad.

Crickets chirp, and the lazy heat of the last bit of summer scorches a tired day into night.

I sit up, looking at Mitchell.

My zombie is much more awake than I am. He stands, and I take in his circa 2010 lumberjack look: scruffy short beard, as inky as the hair on his head, and eyes that rival the rapidly darkening skies that nip at the heels of daylight, chasing it to darkness.

"What happened?" I croak, checking out our new environment.

Mitchell shakes his head slowly, holding out a palm.

I slap mine inside his large warm palm, and three of my fingers twinge.

I wince, remembering that Brad broke them, to bring my family.

Like dogs to heel.

The torture worked—just like it had in bot world when the Brad of that world peeled off three of my nails as I screamed and begged for mercy.

My inhale is shaky, uncertain, but I stand beside Mitchell. I try for calm despite the panic inside me beating like a bird trying to escape a cage.

"Shh… Deegan," Mitchell says, pushing my head against his chest.

"Where are they, Mitchell? Where is my family? Mom, Dad—Pax?"

His dead heart beats against me with a healthy steady rhythm.

"I don't want to make you more upset. But I admit… I don't care."

I pull away, and he lets me. I'm steaming pissed. "Listen, you—those are my family!" I sputter into the still forest, my fearful memories receding for the moment.

"Be quiet, Deegan," Mitchell says, his face darkening.

"I will not!" I bellow.

He slaps a beefy hand over my mouth. The edges of his fingertips tickle my earlobe. And I hear the music of a necklace swinging forward from underneath his flannel shirt.

Mitchell's dark eyes are pockets of shadow in his hard face. "Do you want to be discovered by those bot creepers?"

I haven't heard that last word in years. Tears leak, breaching the dam of his fingers, and I shake my head.

He cautiously lifts his hand. "I would *never* hurt you, Deegan. You have to know that."

Of course I know that. No zombie an AftD raises can hurt us. There's never been a reported case in all the years there've been zombies.

But my ego is bruised. I turn away from Mitchell and watch the sun sink, waiting impatiently for the night so I can see better.

The red ball of the sun sinks like an angry scarlet eye below the Olympic Mountains of this world, spilling its color like discarded blood. The sunset soaks the landscape, spreading tendrils of deep scarlet and orange, with a thread of pink. When the curls of light drown us, the night becomes an ocean of blue. The pungent smell of the forest becomes less as the world cools with the loss of day.

I blink in relief.

My second, thin eyelid covers my eyeballs, and the night comes alive. Everything in my periphery springs before me as though it's daytime, and I see as well at night as I did just before the sun set.

I don't realize I'm holding my breath until it squeezes out of me in a tight sigh.

Mitchell takes my hand. "You can *blink*?"

I nod. "Not like Pax—of course. Just see better."

"That's not a bad thing." His gravelly voice is gentle in my ears.

I smile, and he does too, making me forgive his extreme actions of before. It's a zombie's way. They're natural protectors of the AftD who raises them. I catch sight of something glowing softly inside his mouth.

"What is that?" I point to his lips.

He smiles and leans forward, kissing the finger I pointed with.

"Oh?" I jump back, laughing, my skin heating. "It's a filling? How barbaric!" I whisper-shout.

Mitchell grins broader, and the filling winks in the last vestiges of light. He heaves his shoulder in a shrug. "So? Are we worried about my mouth when we should be looking for the others?"

Yes. *I'm pretty distracted by his mouth.* Especially his lips. I'm instantly glad it's too dark for him to see the blush I'm sure is making my face red.

I punch him on the arm. "Yes—we *should* be looking. Yes, I should be worried." I flutter my fingers. "But my fingers aren't broken, and me not being with anyone but you means my family is relatively safe. Because Brad Thompson and company want me. Those asshat Helix Complex guys want me and Pax, too." But I'm not in my world right now, so at least I don't have to deal with the HC.

Mitchell nods. "Maybe. But your dad—what did he say?"

I fold my arms, tears burning behind my eyelids. For all my talk of their assumed safety, I'm not a hundred percent certain of their fate. Speculation isn't an absolute. It's just a fancy guess. "He said that the HC no longer exists. But those recruiters…."

"The suits whose hands disappeared." Mitchell smirks.

The burn behind my eyelids intensifies, and I burst into tears.

"Whoa," Mitchell says softly, pulling me against his body. "I didn't mean anything by that, Deegan. I think it's great they got the black hole amputation. Handy little talent."

I nod quickly, but a lifetime of not using my black hole ability has caused me debilitating guilt about finally using it. No matter how necessary it was.

"You did what you had to do."

Then why do I feel like shit about it?

Mitchell tips my chin up, making me look at him, his finger a brand of heat against my jaw. "I might be the zombie guy you keep telling me I am, but I know a few things, Deegan."

I swallow. *Can he make me feel less bad about my ability? Can Mitchell do that?*

As though he read my mind, Mitchell says, "I can't take away this disappearing limbs thing you can do"—his lips twist in a smile of irony—"but I make a kickass bodyguard." His dark eyebrows jump. "Or zombieguard."

I burst out laughing.

Mitchell grins, and the expression softens his hard edges.

"Besides," he says with great care, "we're not even in the bot world anyways."

I blink rapidly and step out of his arms. "What?" I ask, going numb.

Mitchell spreads his muscular arms away from his body, and the flannel overshirt he wears stretches over his broad chest.

I zero in on the plaid material. Red. Black. A fine thread of green doesn't escape my perfect night vision.

"Where?" I sputter.

He snorts, though I fail to see anything vaguely humorous. "Somewhere *not* bot."

I move close to him again. "First, how do you know? Second, why don't you know *where*?"

Mitchell catches his chin between his bent pointer knuckle and thumb. Seconds pound by.

"I'm a zombie, right," he says finally, like an explanation.

I can only nod. I raised him. Our irrefutable connection thrums between us like an unseen force.

"I guess the best way to describe it is—the place where I died?" He gives me a sharp glance, clearly wondering if I'm following his train of thought.

"Yes," I say slowly.

"Well, it's like a homing beacon. My body knows where it belongs, and even if I could find the exact place in this world where I died, the ground wouldn't 'receive' me."

Oh shit. Heat floods my skull.

I tumble onto my ass and struggle to put my head between my knees.

Mitchell sinks to his haunches behind me, stroking my back while I hyperventilate.

"Oh my God," I whisper.

"What? Deegan, the suspense is killing me."

I glance up, and his smile is sly.

My zombie's got a sense of humor.

I frown. "Maybe I did too good a job raising you, huh?" I grump.

His smile fades, and I'm instantly pissed I chased away his bit of happiness.

Mitchell begins to rise and I grab his hand, stopping him, though he could easily get away from me.

"I'm sorry. I'm being a bitch."

He doesn't say I'm not.

Ouch.

I recap, trying to move past the awkwardness I accidentally inserted. "What this means is Pax either *blinked* me somewhere different to protect me." I bite my lip, unable to say the next words.

"Or"—Mitchell takes my hands and soothes me with his undead touch, the absolute salve to a person with Affinity for the Dead—"you have what he does."

I feel my forehead tighten into a frown.

Mitchell chuckles, pressing a stray hair behind my ear. "Deegan, I heard someone say your name in the same sentence as *genius*."

I open my mouth to make a smart remark, then press my lips into a tight line. His theory *is* plausible. I just don't want it to be. When we all figured out that our abilities were not necessarily the same on these other parallel dimensions, it was scary. The unknown.

Black hole and *blinking*?

I could make worlds disappear.

Mitchell's face is serious as he studies my expression. He knows when I get the implication because I cover my face with my trembling fingers.

"I don't want to be *more*. I'm already too *much*."

He wipes a stray tear off my face with his thumb, and his hand falls from my face. "I know, Deegan. But sometimes it is what it is. We have to deal even when we don't want to. And cheer up—let's find Pax and the others and send that guy Parker to wherever everyone goes when they get sucked into your black hole."

I peek at him between my fingers, and he's grinning again. *Great.* I have to raise someone whose glass is always half-full.

Mine is usually half-empty.

"You're talking about killing people, Mitchell." My eyes roam over his face, searching for sincerity.

His face goes tight, darker than the night that surrounds his expressive features. "Maybe," he nods slowly, putting a thumb dead center on his muscular chest. "Again—zombie." He raises his hand like a student asking to speak. "I can feel only one directive."

He draws my hand forward, spreading each one of my fingers over his heart. "I know who I must protect—and what happens to those who try to cause harm to my mistress."

My fingers tingle with his words, his touch.

Then Mitchell leans in close to my lips, all heat and breath—the promise of a kiss. "And they'll all die if they touch you, Deegan."

I shake with his nearness, though I'm not cold.

Dad had told me what being AftD entailed. Zombie love wasn't for the faint of heart.

I thought Clyde and Bobbi were an exception. I believed eventually there would be *someone* for me. Even though men my age were scarce in my world since the Helix Complex sterilization implementation, which happened before I was born.

The very thing I hate *being* gave me Mitchell.

Now I have to figure out how to save my family and survive this new world long enough to find out how to get to the world my family's in.

I forget it all, though. My thoughts. My speculations. They leave me like smoke through a crack as Mitchell finishes what he began, pressing his lips to mine.

They're warm—alive.

Though he's dead, he's more alive than anyone I've ever known.

Hands that murdered before he died splay at my lower back, pressing against the dimples that Dad calls angel kisses, and Mitchell groans, his soft lips hard on my mouth.

I open to him.

Mitchell's tongue caresses me. My mouth. My heart. My soul.

When a disembodied voice cuts through our heat, I stumble backward.

Mitchell whirls me around behind him, protectively standing in front of me.

A weapon fires with a soft twang.

Mitchell growls, and time stands still.

A rod with a feathered end zooms toward us, and my gasp is a surprised wheeze.

The sharp end pierces the moist lichen and moss of the forest floor we find ourselves standing in.

The tip isn't an arrow tip. I jump as the end breaks apart, and the half dozen splinters unfold, grabbing the earth. A seventh flicks backward, and a small round mirror, roughly double the size of what a girl might carry in her purse, slips open.

The glass winks, and I see Mitchell and me in the dim reflection it casts.

A tall man with light hair stands five meters away in a dark uniform.

"Who the fuck are you?" Mitchell shouts, dividing his attention between the weird arrow and the man who sprung up out of nowhere.

"At least he's not a bot," I whisper.

The man's sharp light eyes try to find me.

Mitchell pushes me farther behind his body.

But the man shifts his weight, and something iridescent on his chest glitters. I recognize what it is before he vanishes. *A butterfly.* He had a butterfly insignia on his uniform.

Then he's standing in front of us.

I scream. I literally shut my eyes for one second, then he was there before us.

Up close, he's huge.

Mitchell moves one inch, and the man hits Mitchell in the neck. I hear a snap and whirl, running in the opposite direction.

My death energy is leaking all over the place, and it reaches for Mitchell, as it does for all things undead. My unique ability knits his wounds without my express will. For me, the ability to heal the dead is as natural and automatic as breathing.

And I'm breathing so hard as I sprint, I can't get enough oxygen. My lungs burn.

Then the man is on me, grabbing me with a hard hand at my nape.

"No!" I try to wrench from his steely grasp.

"I am sorry. Atomics are not allowed in Papillio."

What? I struggle, writhing like a snake, trying to get away. *Papill-what?*

"Or any world," his sinister voice finishes softly. *He sounds like he's from earth*, I think randomly.

He squeezes.

I yelp, still thrashing.

"Sleep," he says.

And I'm not tired. *I have to get to Mitchell. Pax! My parents.*

My eyes disobey me. They shut, though I've never wanted to be awake more than I do in that moment.

Slumber comes, stealing my consciousness like a thief.

2

Pax

"Where's Sister?"
I hear the question vaguely, as if I'm underwater.

Shake—roll. Somebody's hand is on my shoulder, rattling my teeth.

What the fuck is this?

My eyes pop open. Well, one eye does; the other one isn't cooperating. It feels like a golf ball of flame and misery.

Someone's elbow nailed me, I guess. *Beautiful.*

I roll my good eye toward the small figure dangling over me.

Mom. I shut my eye then open it again. Jade Hart's black hair tickles my nose, and I flick it out of my face as her hand drops from my shoulder.

"Mom—*God.* Let me get my bearings, would ya?"

Mom's lips quirk, but she steps backward. Dad slowly comes into focus beside her.

Wait. A. Second.

Brad Thompson. Fake Parkers. *Real* Parkers.

I swim off my back with flailing arms then stagger to standing—grab the nearest person to keep from falling on my ass again.

Gramps rights my drunken stumble. Except—here's the fun—*not drunk*. "Whoa, Pax—steady."

I blink. Not the cool kind of *blink* that will jettison us to parts unknown, but the kind that soothes the eyes.

"Where are we?" I ask with a mouth that feels like it's filled with dog shit and marbles. My throat clicks as I attempt to swallow.

I take in the landscape. It's a beaut, I admit.

"Looks like we're in a new world, son." Caleb Hart—aka Dad—raises a dark-brown eyebrow.

I get the message loud and clear. *Where the fuck are we, and where is Dee?*

Here's the deal: *I don't know where Dee is.* I don't know where the bad guys are.

Situation fucked.

I inhale deeply, cough on the way out, and notice a city below us. On first glance, it looks very old-fashioned. Like Rome. The Rome I've seen in pictures anyway.

Okaaay.

Scratch that. Situation is definitely fucked *and* unknown.

"Gramps," I say in a hollow voice. Feels like I've been scooped out and put back together backward.

"Yeah?" he answers, patting down the front of his Poindexter shirt. "I could use a smoke about now. Yup."

I turn slowly.

Gramps winks, looking lost without a cig jammed between his lips. "Got a shiner, Pax. It's a beauty."

Thanks for stating the obvious.

"Gramps, please," Dad says, surveying our current disaster.

"Honey—Pax—where'd you *blink* Sister to."

Hell if I know.

Mom's face is pinched and miserable.

Damn. "Not sure, Mom, but let's look at the good news."

"Oh yeah, pal? What's that? Dying to have some good news. Hell, Caleb breezes by the hood, and wham—I'm right back in the weirdness."

I turn to Jonesy. The Jonester. Jones. I don't know—I think his real name is actually Mark. Never heard anyone call him that, though. Oh yeah, Dad's burglar friend, Lewis Archer never gets called by his first name either.

I shake my head. My life is *not* normal.

My one good eye makes progress, scoping out green rolling hills. The sun is sinking for the day, like a dying crimson orb. Like spilt blood, it's creeping over the buildings of what looks like ancient Rome, placed about where Kent, Washington, would be on our earth.

Not any Kent I've ever seen, though. I point at the place, which is flanked by field upon field of grapes.

Clyde moves forward, coming to stand beside me. "I no longer feel you, young master."

My chest tightens like a brutal tug of fishing line, and I automatically send out my death energy. *There isn't any.*

Fuck. Me.

I face Clyde.

Dad strides to me, holding Mom's hand tightly in his. "What?" His eyes scan my face.

"Do you have AftD here, Dad?"

"Yes." No hesitation. Then his brows dump above chocolate-colored eyes. "You don't?"

"Not a drop."

"Well, that blows," Tiff comments.

I cock an eyebrow.

Tiff Weller grins.

Show off.

The semi-long pasture grass on the knoll overlooking the buildings below begins to undulate. Dead garter snakes wrestle the emerald-green blades apart, slithering toward Tiff. She's flexing her Affinity for the Dead muscle.

Tiff's eyes meet first Dad's, then Clyde's.

Dad puts his hands on his hips—his version of a thinking cap, eyebrow cocked at the snake parade. "The thugs haven't shown up yet. I propose we progress with caution. Knowing our skills…" Dad's gaze ping-pongs around the new digs, and he finally says, "Rome world," then chuckles, "would be better than heading down there." He tosses his thumb in the direction of the city below us, "And no one knows if the natives are friendly."

I like that. But we don't have enough knowledge to even go forward. Where's Dee? Better yet, where's her pet zombie, Mitchell? "I don't like my absent AftD."

Jonesy claps me on the back. "Hey, man, thought you hated being a corpse-boy?" He waggles his brows.

Dad gives a little shake of his head.

Yeah. Right. Jones of the No-Filter variety. Gotcha. "I like it fine when the shit hits the fan."

"Language," Clyde cautions softly.

John ignores my sullen bullshit. "Let's be exclusionary."

All eyes turn to him, and I do a speedy head count. Tiff and John Weller. One AftD and a Null. Dad, who still has AftD, and Mom, with whatever *she* has in Rome world. Sophie, Archer, and Bry are all unknowns. And Parker—both Parkers—are MIA.

"John," Sophie says with unhidden irritation, aqua eyes flashing, "let's get the ball rolling. I'm super hungry, and my feet are killing me."

Everyone looks at Sophie's feet. She's wearing really stupid sparkly purple leopard-print flats. Super-pointy toes. Fashion looks painful.

Sophie stares back. "Hey," she says defensively, stabbing upward with her finger, "I didn't get up this morning and go, 'Oh, I'm going to interdimensionally travel, so I better where ugly shoes.'" She slaps her thighs, having perched on a sand-colored boulder.

I'm tallying paranormal skills, and Sophie's worried about food and footwear.

I toss Dad a look, and he shrugs. My face says clearly, *"You survived this?"*

His features arrange a sheepish expression.

So lame.

"Actually, Soph, it's not a dimensional thing."

Dad looks at John Terran and folds his arms across his chest. "John, no time for lessons."

Uncle John shakes his head. "I agree with Paxton."

I brighten. *He does?* Fucking great.

Tiff pops a massive bubble, startling me and Mom. "Sorry," she says, noticing she made us jump out of our skins, "but it keeps the booze at bay."

Great.

Gramps smirks, and John's face turns red.

John tries to ignore Tiff—no small thing—and continues, "This world hopping—*blinking*—that Pax executes? It's more of a parallel-world *shift*."

"John!" Sophie cries indignantly.

He sighs. "Listen, if it was simply dimensional travel, there'd be a certain number of worlds. What Pax is doing is going to a world that has an infinite number of its own parallels."

Jonesy gives a slow blink. "Right. So… how does knowing that help us?"

John scrubs his face. "Doesn't anyone ever want to know the *why?*"

Archer raises his hand. "I enjoy backstory. However, John, I think we should ruminate on escape and avoidance at this juncture, rather than thinking about all the possibilities of inner-world travel."

"I don't give a shit," Jones says, then turns to Uncle John. "I dig you, my man—I do. But you kinda delve when we should just dive." Jonesy mimes the breaststroke.

"Cripes, Jonesy," Dad says, shaking his head, though he can't hide the smile.

"What?" He spins slowly, and the snakes that Tiff raised rotate, making the grass look as though a breeze has kicked up, but only at shin level. "I'm with Soph"—he pats his flat stomach—"gotta fuel up."

"Man-whoring must burn a buttload of calories," Sophie retorts in a sullen voice, chin in her palm.

Shit. Pissed woman alert.

"We're getting off track," John puts up a hand.

Jonesy narrows his eyes on Sophie.

Tiff barks, "Jonesy!"

"What!" He dances away from the snakes, figuring they're the issue.

When I see what's shown up, I realize that Archer might be right. *Should have focused on the priorities right away.*

The dead stand a few meters away, regarding us. Waiting.

Their eyes ignore me. A first. I'm usually The Shit with the dead. I crook my finger, and they come running. Or shambling. It's all the same.

They come.

But their eyes aren't on me. They're on Jonesy.

"Oh, this is a treasure," Gramps says in a caustic tone.

Clyde's head snaps to Jonesy, who titters a laugh as he retreats a step from the tight little horde he unwittingly raised. "What is this slice of strange? Hart!" Jonesy calls.

Dad steps forward, Tiff and Clyde flanking him. "Looks like we've fleshed out *your* ability on this world." Dad's voice is Sahara Desert dry.

Jonesy puts both palms on his chest. "No way, man! The Jonester refuses to be a corpse-man."

I feel the grin split my face. *Sometimes life is so fine.* I don't want AftD, and neither does Jones. I just passed the baton. Sweet.

The dead shamble forward, and I give the rotting group a once-over. "Really a shit job, Jones," I say with a critical eye.

Dad turns, giving me a *silence* look. "He got the mouths, son," he says, his tone admonishing me.

I look back. Yup, all those yawning holes are pink. Then a few teeth fall out as one of the corpses actually does a pulsevision-worthy moan.

I've never heard a zombie make that sound in my short life.

"Hart—they don't seem right. They're straight from that pulse flick from the last century."

Really? We're discussing cinema?

"*Shaun of the Dead*," Bry pipes in for the first time. "Loved that show. British. Tight. Dry as fuck with the humor."

"Language," Clyde says again with slightly less vim and vigor.

"Sorry, Clyde," Bry says.

"Not to worry, my profane friend."

Our eyes meet those of the corpses and for the first time. I'm afraid.

Dad frowns. "Jones, you're like a guy at the wheel of a car."

Jonesy turns, giving Dad a grimace like a slash of white in the dark skin of his face. "Is this the ten-second *how to* on reanimation?"

Dad nods, not bothering with sugar-coated words.

Jonesy whips his face back. "Hurry up, Hart. They're almost on my dick."

Sophie snorts.

"I really need a smoke for this," Gramps comments. "Jonesy corpses—bad. Very bad."

I silently agree.

"If your control isn't absolute, they're like a rudder, and with you at the helm, I think your personality might just steer them in an undesirable direction," John says the words to Jonesy, but his eyes are on the dead.

"Caleb," Mom says.

Dad nods. "I'll help."

I shake my head. What? Did Dad forget the quintessential 101 of zombie raising?

Only the raiser is in charge.

"Rest," Dad begins in a resonate command.

I'm basically an AftD void in this world, but even I feel the weight of his power. His single spoken word lifts the fine hairs at my nape.

That'll do it.

The zombies, maybe a dozen in all, blink. The yawner of the group hisses at Dad, who frowns.

Gramps cracks his knuckles. "Things are getting pear-shaped, Caleb."

Dad's brows meet. "Yeah, I got that, Gramps."

"Can't fix it?"

Dad shakes his head. "They're only on one frequency."

All head's turn to Jonesy, including a few that make wet, snapping noises with the movement.

"Stop playing around, Jonesy, and put all these nasty asses in the ground," Sophie says, her fingers over her nose.

Jonesy turns to her. "Do you think for one second I wanted Team Undead to show up?"

Sophie sticks out her lip in an expert pout. "You're an attention whore, too." She folds her arms.

Lots of sour history there, I'm guessing. No time for that now. The rot is reaching my acute olfactory senses, and my fight-or-flight instincts are on full throttle. Time to vacate and find Dee.

"Jonesy, just make them go to ground," I state logically.

"How, wise one?"

I jerk my chin back. *It's easy, just...* My mind goes blank. I have no AftD here. It's impossible to explain. My smile is fixed on my face like it's stuck with bad glue. "Dad, tell Jonesy how to get the dead back."

Dad's eyebrows jerk to his hairline just as the first zombie puts a loving fingertip on Jonesy's face.

"Argh!" Jonesy wails like a pirate on crack, leaping backward. Zombie slime drips off the edge of his chin.

We all take a collective step back. Somehow, my own corpses don't bug me—but somebody else's? Different story.

"Looks like they're *in love*, Jones," Bry says conversationally.

Jonesy flicks the zombie sludge off his chin with a disgusted grunt. "Fuck you, Weller."

Clyde doesn't chastise on language, because just at that precise moment a pair of people pop out of thin air.

The very space around them is charged with electricity. But not like they've stuck their fingers in one of those outdated light sockets from the pre-pulse days.

No. Like ozone from the ocean. Crackling iridescent sparkles explode around them, and the memory of a smoking ribbon burns my corneas.

There's one guy and one girl. The man is huge; the woman is the polar opposite. About Dee's size, I figure. Both have the look of soldiers.

Whatever they are, they mean business. Kind of like our sanction police from earth.

"Sector Three," the male says. His dark-blond hair is sheared close to his scalp, above disconcerting eyes almost the same color as Archer's gray gaze. But where Archer's are cotton tinged by pewter, this guy's are the threat of a storm. They bleed malice over the top of us.

The woman is dark, and her hair is fashioned in tight braids laying flat against her head. Her hair's like Dee's, black like a crow's wing, but where Dee's got forest green eyes, this chick's are so dark brown that they hide her pupil. Their contrast against the pale-ivory of her skin is startling.

"Death Bringers," she replies to the male by her side. Her face swings to Jonesy, Tiff, then Dad. "One. Two. Three."

The male snorts. "Easily dealt with."

"What are they speaking? You know, I'm getting sick and tired of never understanding what anyone is saying," Gramps says, pawing his shirt pocket again.

I whip my face to his. "You don't know?" My eyes travel the group. They're as blank as Gramps.

"Some kind of ancient-sounding Spanish," Uncle John pipes up.

I understood every word.

When the male utters the word for *kill*, I do what I must.

"Hands!" I bellow.

No twenty questions on that command. Palms slap inside one another.

Twilight descended twenty minutes ago. I *blink*.

The girl's eyes round as her image wavers in front of me. A smile stretches her face, and for a split-second, I believe she might have been pretty if she weren't so tough.

She throws something in the air with a practiced wrist flick. The spinning disc shimmers.

My own eye appears on the smooth surface for a fraction of one second of its midair revolution.

Then we disappear from the Rome world and the accidental zombies. Leaving behind the soldiers who identified everyone who had AftD.

Or so we thought.

3

Deegan

I sit straight up, my heart pounding. The base of my skull throbs where that man gripped me.

Looking around, I notice about half a dozen prison-type cells. Narrow deeply set windows are high on the stone walls. Ceramic bars obstruct a flat, clear acrylic pane instead of glass. The floor is a smooth surface. It's very similar to the recycled quartz of my world.

The same ceramic bars blocking the squatty windows also cage me in on three sides; the stone wall is rough and cool at my back.

"Ah, there you are. Wakey-wakey."

I'm woozy and disoriented. But being pissed really helps clear my head.

The man that caused me to pass out pushes off with a foot from the gray stone wall that faces opposite my position. I am in the cell; he is outside.

That's the upside.

He told me to go to sleep. *Manipulator,* I think with a bite of terror. Manipulators no longer exist in my world.

My situation has become even worse than it was. I dump Brad Thompson—and certain future zombie manipulation and torture—so I can be dropped into the lap of this jerk.

Figures. Murphy's Law is just *everywhere.*

The current A-hole moves toward me like a big prowling cat. Fear climbs my throat. I whip my head around, hoping for an easy escape. *There's nothing simple in this place.*

I face my captor again.

Mitchell is nowhere. Tears cling to my already-wet eyeballs, threatening to fall.

The uniform that had appeared almost black in the dimness of the woods is actually a very dark blue. Navy. The insignia of an iridescent butterfly is like a lie above his heart. Nothing that pretty could be reserved for a dude who puts a girl to sleep and breaks my zombie's neck. He can dress as beautifully as he wants; the shell doesn't hide his evilness.

His eyes are soulless.

The man before me could be considered handsome by most. His smile is bright, but false. He's tall, as big as Pax, and built like a Body. I glance at his hands, remembering how large the one he wrapped the back of my neck was. How murderous.

His name is etched above the glittering insect. *Ryan.*

I try to move my arms and realize I'm tied. I wiggle my fingers and still have sensation.

A relieved exhale shudders out of me. *Not very much time has passed.*

Happy birthday, Deegan. Again.

Ryan finishes his stroll across the room and comes to stand in front of my cell. If it can be called a cell. The bars are some kind of slightly opaque porcelain. They don't look like they would hold up against much.

I start plotting. I'm a Hart, after all.

"They cannot be broken," he says as if he's psychic.

But I don't think he is. Just a good guesser. He doesn't give off that in-your-brain-slime feel I get from telepaths.

I gulp.

He's a little older than I am, but he's so hard that he wears his skin like flint-covered steel, instantly aging himself with his demeanor.

I flex my fingers again. "Why am I being held prisoner? Is it against the law to be in the woods?"

His unnervingly light eyes are oblique seawater, weighing me—and clearly find me lacking. His expression shifts to amusement, and Ryan clasps his hands behind his back. He moves like a soldier, or what police might be in this place, but he's *off.* What he did to me and Mitchell is wrong.

That would be easy to figure no matter what world Pax *blinked* me to.

"No," he says, the word clipped. "You have violated no laws. However, you are a Three, and as such, have lost your way." His lips curl with some kind of private amusement he doesn't share.

My breaths become shorter. Somehow, I don't like where this is headed. Call it a feeling. "What's a 'Three'?"

"Earth. *Your* earth. Sector Three," he says like he's speaking to a child. His attitude incites my ire.

I am a numbered IQ. Only genius-level people have a number. I can navigate most circumstances pretty well. Even other-world circumstances. "I'm not confused, just ignorant. I was doing nothing wrong."

He spreads his palms away from his body. "Except existing."

I frown and say in a quiet voice, "I have a right to live."

Ryan chuckles. "Maybe your earth allows an Atomic—though I do not know how they would contain such a skill. They do not possess immunity as Reflectives do."

Atomic.

I remember he called me that. *Before.* Before he gave me the whammy.

"You can cause things to be removed from all planes of existence."

Black hole. He means my black hole ability. *Atomic.* Science springs a leak inside my head. Atoms. Atomic level. Black hole. *Ah.*

"Yeah. So?" I glare.

"So. She says 'so.'" His chuckle is dark, his hands fists. Veins bulge like a ribbon on his muscular forearms where he's rolled up his dark-blue uniform sleeves. "It is not *so*. We police against your kind."

There's no reasoning with this guy. He's had a slice of the crazy pie. "Just let me and Mitchell go." I try for nice, adding a plea to my tone. "We can go back to…" I scurry for his words where they hide in the crevices of my still-fuzzy brain. "Three."

Ryan shakes his head. "No."

My heartbeats stack like Jenga blocks.

"Besides which, your undead pet has been subdued."

No, no, no… *no!* "What did you do to Mitchell?" I yell. Spittle dots my lips, pain roaring at the base of my neck.

His eyes darken to glacial-caressed rage. "Yelling is unbecoming of a lady."

I suck in my next breath like a lifeline. "Fuck you," I grind out.

Ryan's condescending smile slips. "I do not have to take you before council, or even our Commander Rachett. After all, I was by myself when I stumbled upon you and your undead. There is no partner to coerce silence from." He makes a disgusted noise in the back of his throat, sounds like he's choking on a loogie.

"Death Bringer *and* Atomic." Ryan snorts, shaking his head in clear disdain.

The AftD is obvious to anyone who has eyes. Mitchell. *Duh.* Somehow Ryan knows I can do black holes. *Atomic,* I correct myself. I'm developing a clear and shining hatred for Ryan, but I like his word better.

Why would he know? My eyes become slits on him. "What are you?"

His smile is immediate and arrogant. Ryan glances to the left of me, and I turn my head to follow the direction of his stare. A small mirror stands in the corner of my all-stone cell.

I frown, not understanding the importance of the mirror. Then a clear image of that strange arrow-type weapon landing in front of me comes to the surface of my addled brain.

He used a mirror then. Before he captured us.

The glass inside the small square winks at me. The mossy-green of my eyeball fills the slightly convex surface.

My brain reconciles the facts, putting together the dots like a constellation of stars. A moment too late.

Then Ryan is inside the cell.

I startle with a yip, throwing myself backward, and Ryan grabs me by the scruff of my neck a second time, hauling me up roughly. Tension and pain sing down my spine.

He gives me serious perusal, his cold eyes missing nothing. "I am a Reflective, you strange creature."

My palms dampen.

I don't know what a Reflective is, but his jumping around using mirrors makes me want to puke on him. *Screw motion sickness.* I'm going *Atomic* on his ass. My long-standing guilt tries to insert itself and can't quite manage it.

Survival of the fittest, Gramps would say.

My eyes shift to his crotch. *I'll start with his teeny weeny penis.* The energy swells inside me, right beneath my breastbone, warming my insides like slow-burning embers.

Ryan's eyes widen.

Then an invisible wall is erected, and the fingers of my little-used power try to peel the unseen force back.

Nothing.

Sweat builds on my upper lip.

Ryan grins and shakes me so hard, my teeth rattle.

My power bursts between us like an out-of-control whip, carving a swath of keening blackness.

The surge of ebony sweeps through Ryan and takes out a wedge of ceramic bars. They wink out of existence and disappear wherever the crap I zap away goes.

Ryan still stands before me, smiling. "You can't manipulate my energy. I'm born naturally."

The ceramic bars' amputated ends smolder at the tips where they once stood as straight and perfect rods.

He shakes me.

My head jerks back and forth. This weirdo is immune?

Fine. Immune *this.*

I send out a death command so pure, it causes slippage in my brain.

I hope I raised a prison of ax murderers.

Ryan grimaces as the summons washes over him. His open hand connects with my chin, spinning me into the jagged stone wall.

My shoulder pounds against the rough rock, and I slide down the wall, hands useless because they're tied against me.

My mind shrieks for the undead. But Ryan comes for me. Not like he's worried—like he's sure.

My heart rate goes nuclear. My breaths are merciless wounds of deprived oxygen as I flatten myself against the textured stone surface.

Mitchell moves into my line of sight behind Ryan. His neck is canted to his shoulder.

His eyes blink at me. Deep, like a bruised sky at midnight.

Zombies don't feel pain. *But I do.*

Tears roll down my face like heated pathways of fear and anguish.

I'm so sorry, Mitchell.

Then he removes something from his pocket.

Ryan pivots faster than a cat, and Mitchell chucks a folded leather thing at the mirror in a leaning sweep. Pretty hard to hit a target when your head's wedged against your shoulder.

I shut my eyes, miserable to the core.

Glass tinkles to the ground beside my body like shards of musical notes.

My eyes tear open, and I meet Mitchell's gaze the moment before Ryan launches at him.

Heal, my mind implores, and every bit of death energy I have left pours into Mitchell.

His lips part in a sigh, his hands going to his skull. Mitchell jerks his head upright. Pops and cracks of vertebrae light like firecrackers in the close space. The bones realign as Ryan crashes into him.

Mitchell grabs the arm that shoves him, using Ryan's limb to spin my captor high and wide.

Fierce satisfaction grips me as my zombie employs that superior strength against this smooth freak.

Ryan smashes into the wall opposite the one I lean against, cracking his skull and smacking palms against the unforgiving stone.

"You only broke one mirror," Ryan gasps out of a chest without air.

Mitchell smirks. "Buzz around like a fly—see how many fucks I give." He smiles, and I see the murderer he was in his face.

The murderer he is now.

Ryan zaps in his own way. Not my power, but something similar. Using the mirrors that remain in the other cells, he tap dances around my fearless zombie.

He takes chunks out of Mitchell as I watch. *He's winning,* I weep inside my battered skull.

I need Pax! *I need more dead.*

My brain splits. Healing every wound Ryan inflicts on my zombie while I call others is something I don't have the finesse for. I'm getting sloppy. I don't have the control.

I don't know what I'll raise here.

Criminals? Or good people.

At least I still have AftD.

The death rush fills me like a cup spilling over. Too late, because they're coming now. I attempt to twist my position, but my butt bones protest. My shoulders burn. The horrible ties abrade my wrists.

When the crows hop down the stairs, they fill the bottom like an dark army.

Ryan jerks the knife out of Mitchell's flank and turns to face the flock. The obsidian blade he carries is dull. Deadly.

I narrow my vision on the newest wound against Mitchell that doesn't bleed. The split sides knit, coming together like a neat line, healing to perfection.

Mitchell steps away from Ryan, his gaze meeting the crows'. Communion. The dead with the dead.

Ryan is clearly unnerved. His large body is poised and ready. His eyes slide from the dead I called to the dead man who murdered those who harmed his family before either of us were born.

Mitchell was more than just a pincushion for Ryan's blows and stabs. He'd destroyed the mirrors as he spun around the jail, expertly avoiding Ryan.

Now there are none.

Ryan's teeth clench as those hard icy bluish-green eyes tear around the space, searching for a shard—anything—to work his evil hopping.

Mitchell backs up.

The crows sweep their wings together, just enough to flit a few meters closer to Ryan.

A crow in the front cocks its head then caws. An achingly vile sound erupts from his throat. The noise is so clear and warlike, it can't be mistaken for anything else.

I entreat my will.

The pecking begins.

Even though I know Ryan meant my certain death, I let Mitchell untie my arms and carry me from the bowels of a prison in an unknown earth, without a single glance in Ryan's screaming direction.

4

Gramps

I lie flat on my back. Clouds like white bullets scoot overhead, piercing an impossibly blue sky.

I'm too old for this shit. And I don't have any smokes. That means I have to deal with everything with no buffer.

Love a good cigarette.

I palm the soft grass on either side of me and sit up, taking in my surroundings.

We're in another world. Well, we're wherever my barely twenty-year-old great-grandson flung us to this time.

I grunt. *Kid's gotta organize his skill set.*

And where the blue hell is Deedie? That pisses me off. *Keep track of your sister*, I say.

I stand, taking a deep breath, hold it, and let it out nice and slow. New lung's standing up well, despite my daily abuse of nicotine and proven carcinogens.

I catch sight of Caleb dusting off his pants and giving Jade a hand up. Then I scan the rest of the semi-comatose bodies lying around in various states of wakefulness.

Rough damn landing. Again.

I chuckle, thinking of Jonesy being AftD. Then I shudder. *Jonesy—AftD. God bless it all.*

I'm stiffer than a plank. Placing the flat of my hand to my lower back, I twist slowly to get the kinks out. Rejuvenation is great, but it doesn't cure all my ills.

"Gramps," Pax says, standing directly to my left.

"Yeah." I drop my hand and turn.

Pax looms over me. *Kid's so goddamned big.* I shake my head. Maybe he's still a Body here? That would be a good stroke of luck.

"We're missing people."

I cast my eyes to the ground, putting my hands on my hips. A little discipline would be nice. Or, screw that—how about a little finesse? I rein in my impatience and jerk my chin up, doing a head count. We got the Wellers (Good damned thing, too. Tiff is a mouthy drunk, but I think we're going to need her brand more than ever). My eyes light on Clyde, the kids, Sophie, Jonesy, and—no Archer or Bry.

Hmm… Ranks have slimmed, but the carload of assholes hasn't made an appearance yet. Silver lining and all that happy crap. "Maybe they slipped through the earth cracks." I cackle.

Pax frowns.

I explain, "Y'know, you let the dead weight go back to Kent." I lift my eyebrows in what I assume is a hopeful expression.

"Gramps"—his tone is irritated, which gets my dander up—"I don't know *where* they are, and I need to find Dee to know where Parker is. That's what's critical. I can't look for the spares."

Spares? Like tires? "What do you mean by that, son?"

Caleb and Jade arrive. Jade has blades of grass stabbing out of her black hair.

"I mean my control of *blinking* isn't that great."

Clearly. I spread my palms, urging him to go on. I'm thinking we need to abandon ship before that dim bulb Thompson and his corrupt Parker sprout like weeds and pull another handy little snafu out of their collective asses.

I glance around, weighing our options. The place with the ruined city is closer now, after this latest whip around. Looks like Pax blinked us not far from the original position but on the same world. *A pure panic move.*

The air around me, sweet with a smell that reminds me of spring, appears to grow, then a shimmering ripple cracks through the space that just felt full to bursting, momentarily blinding me with an iridescent rope of moving light.

The man and woman from before form instantly.

Pax reacts immediately, punching the man in the throat.

I sigh in resignation. *Game on.*

He catches Pax's arm before it lands and twists it between his shoulder blades.

"Pax!" Caleb roars then sets the guy's feet on fire in the middle of pasture land in Weird World.

Swell.

"What the righteous fuck?" Jonesy bellows like a well-timed alarm. His zombies turn their heads toward the new offenders.

Oh? We somehow *blinked* the horde? I snort an abrupt chuckle. "Gotta do everything myself," I mutter, lurching my way into the melee.

The woman gets in close to her partner's cooking feet and tries to smother the flames.

"Sorry, missy," I say with real regret, then thunk her on the back of the head.

She doesn't respond as I hoped—by cooperatively blacking out. Instead, she clocks me in the jaw for my trouble.

Legs splayed, I fall directly on my ass with a teeth rattling clap. *God bless it.*

"I am sorry, elder," she replies apologetically. But her eyes glint with humor.

No problem. Let me get handed my ass by a girl in a navy-blue uniform with a butterfly insignia. *I love when that happens,* I think with morose glee, tipping backward onto the pasture grass.

I lie on my back for the second time, the smell of smoke and burning rubber singing my nostrils, and wonder for the umpteenth time why I volunteer to go on these little excursions.

Oh yeah, Mac O'Brien doesn't turn down a challenge.

That thought pops my wily ass back into the fray, and I scramble to a stand, head spinning. I get enough wind in the gullet to breathe and take in the scene before me.

The little lady is a whirling cyclone of limbs. She's laid out John and Jonesy, and she's working on Caleb.

Not to be undone, Clyde wades in, bellowing about "master" and that.

Truth is, the girl is just that deadly.

Pax and the man, his feet smoking to beat the band, are toe to smoldering toe.

The guy pounds Pax in the chest with a shove that sends him flying through the air before he lands in a crumpled pile of limbs and wounded ego.

"Well this is a class-A clusterfuck." This from Tiff, eloquent as always.

She's righter than rain on that score.

Jonesy says, "Sick 'em!"

The zombies begin their sloppy shamble toward the man and woman.

Jesus, Mary, and Joseph. I stick my fingers in the sides of my mouth and give an eardrum-bursting whistle. The noise pierces the heavens with a bell-like insistence, shattering silence and arresting everyone mid-punch.

Haven't blasted one of those suckers out in forever.

The two strangers in matching uniforms straighten, looking at the rest of us with deserving caution. Their gazes linger a second or two longer on the tight rotting horde Jonesy barely has under control.

Can't fault them for hesitating with the undead around.

I raise my hand. "Hi, other-worlders." I would give my eye teeth for a smoke, but instead, I grin like a loon at the pair who're soundly kicking our asses. "Do ya think you could not kill us long enough to let us ask a few questions?"

They blink simultaneously, and that strikes me as funny. The hell with the crooked mouth that Caleb is always struggling with. I give a belly laugh that if I'm not careful, will morph into something edgier and not quite good.

I chance a glance at the rotting group and note they're mid-stumble to the pair. *Hmmm…*

All that malarkey about getting older is the God's honest truth. It sucks, and then you die.

"Anyone volunteering?" I ask to the general crowd.

Oops. Pax, John, and Jonesy are rolling around groaning on the grass. "Nice representatives, assjacks," I mutter.

The woman cocks her head and says something to her partner. I'm afraid she might have heard that last.

Be that as it may, I walk over there, and as I get closer, I watch the bruises a few of the guys landed on Big Guy begin to heal.

Well we're not in Kansas anymore, Toto. Mhhmm.

The woman is small, like Deedie, and has black hair like hers, as well. But her eyes are jet black. They move to meet me. Unflinching. Cool.

"You two speak English?" I swing my pointer finger between the two.

The woman steps forward, and I take a cautious step back. I've seen her in action—I won't go up against her and win. Kinda fond of my balls. She looks like that'd be the number one strike.

"Assume their diction, Jasper. Otherwise, it will seem too formal."

Surprise, surprise.

The female assassin rolls her eyes at the guy then directs that dark gaze at me. "I am Beth Jasper."

"I'm Mac O'Brien."

She tilts her head at the same time she flicks a long braid over her shoulder. "This is my partner, Jeb Merrick."

I study the man for a full minute and finally stick out my hand to be shaken.

Or cut off.

"We are well met," Jeb Merrick says, dropping my hand after a painful one-two pump.

I feel my brows corkscrew.

Jasper sighs, her brow wrinkling. "I will speak for us."

Merrick's jaw flutters, but he stays silent.

So not everything is rosy in their relationship. Noted. I fold my arms.

Beth Jasper spreads her arms away from her body. "You are from Three."

My eyebrows shoot up. Three-*what*?

"Sector Three." Her nose scrunches in her small face. "We are Reflectives. How is it that you find yourself in our sector?"

I look around for Pax. Jade is with him, hovering over his wounds.

The bruises and cuts Merrick inflicted begin to heal. So he's still Organic enough to fix himself. Good.

I jerk a thumb over my shoulder. "Grandkid here can jump around different worlds." I shrug. *I don't know how to explain all the paranormal crap. I just work here.*

"Merrick." She tenses a little when he is already at her side.

His cold steel-colored eyes fall on me.

They start speaking that gibberish again.

I throw up my palms. "Hey, guys, stop with the foreign-speak. Plain old English, or this little convo is *finito*."

Their gazes swing to look at me. "Who is your grandchild?"

Pax raises a hand from the ground. "Me." He jerks his head off the grass, lasering in on Merrick. "The one you were trying to kill."

Merrick's lips curl, and he chuckles. The expression is the first thing he's wore on his face besides a perpetual scowl. "If I were trying, you would even now be dead."

Pax's head falls back on the grass, but he raises his arm, presenting the bird for old Reflective Blondie.

Merrick glares at Pax in repose.

I chuckle. *That kid.*

Caleb claps me on the back. "He sounds like the sphere-world people."

I snap my fingers—the accent was tickling the back of my brain every time Merrick would speak.

"Sphere-world?" he asks.

Jasper says, "I think he means sector Thirteen."

Merrick tips his head back. "Ah."

"Thirteen?" Caleb asks.

"The world of spheres," Jasper elaborates.

Cleared my confusion right up. *Pfft.*

Jonesy snorts, voicing my thoughts aloud. "That makes sense. Thanks, guys."

The zombies shift. A wafting reek of rot reaches me. I smile.

"God!" Sophie flops back down on a rock, assuming her prior version of bored, and slams her chin inside her cupped palm.

"I'd like to know who you are and why you can," Jade says quietly, making a back-and-forth motion with her palm.

"We are the... police of thirteen sectors—worlds. My partner and I are born Reflectives."

Uh-huh. Nutbunnies.

"What's a Reflective?" John asks.

Tiff pops a bubble so loud, it's a small bomb in the field, and everyone jumps, including the Reflectives, who crouch, arms wide and hands loose by their sides.

They look to Tiff and straighten from their defensive postures.

"What is she doing with her mouth?" Merrick asks, momentarily distracted.

"I think it's called chewing gum," Jasper replies, a small frown ruining the perfection of her forehead.

The corner of Merrick's lips tweak. "And she would eat that for sustenance?"

"It's just something to calm my nerves, guys. Get over yourselves."

Merrick's lips pull away from his teeth in what I suppose passes for his version of a smile. "Foul disposition."

They have no idea.

Tiff grunts. "Yeah. Whatevers, Reflection Wonder Twins."

"Tiff," John says in a low voice.

"No, I like it," Jonesy says, obviously in the moment. "I want answers, and they're asking about gum." He glances at his zombies, and they move forward a stride.

Merrick's face has changed expression several times. The one he wears now is a perfect combo of contempt and irritation, with a dash of unease (probably those corpses give a fella pause). He opens his mouth to comment, clearly thinks better of it, and turns to John. "A

Reflective is a person…" He pauses, and I notice how Jasper stiffens slightly when Merrick says the word *person*. "A person who is born with the ability to Reflect. We then travel to other primary worlds to ensure justice and sustainability."

"Huh," Tiff says, popping another bubble.

How does she *have gum?* I'm grumpy about my lack of cigarettes.

John pinches the bridge of his nose, his eyes lighting on the small disc secured to Jasper's belt. "You use inanimate objects that possess reflective material."

The Reflectives nod.

"You hop between worlds?" John presses.

They incline their heads at the same moment, looking like the bizarre twins Tiff accused them of being.

John strokes his chin. "Why did you attack us?"

"We did not attack you. You attacked us."

I frown. *Had us there.* Pax had delivered the blow that started the brawl.

"I heard you say 'kill,'" Pax says, warily joining the conversation.

Merrick grins, and the expression utterly changes his face from serious stick-up-your-ass to approachable human being. "Not *to* kill you. But to save you from *being* killed. There are a few…" Merrick pauses, as though thinking of his next words carefully. "Skills"—his light eyes find mine, then each one of the others'—"which are not allowed on Papilio."

We stare back blankly.

"*Animators a mortuis* are not allowed. Death Bringers. It is illegal to exist in Papilio with this ability." Jasper raises her chin, as if willing us to defy her. "It is not safe for you here." She glances at Caleb, Tiff, and Jonesy. Jasper's smile is sudden, fierce. "Thank Principle you do not have an Atomic within your numbers, or any of us would be honor-bound to clean that human, regardless of world of origin. At the very least, he or she would be called before council."

Pax turns to me. The words he'll say begin to form in my mind. I know it'll be a bad *a-ha* moment.

I'm not disappointed.

"What's an Atomic?" Pax asks with slow deliberation. He's just like his dad, when the wheels are turning.

"Oh," Jasper says, waving it away, "I have never encountered such an ability. I mentioned it only as an example. We do know the ability exists. Atomics have been documented in the course of history."

The group gives her more blank face.

Jasper, more patient than Merrick, answers, "An Atomic is someone who can manipulate matter."

"Make crap disappear?" Pax's voice is a thread of sound.

Jasper inclines her head in a sage nod. "That is the least of what such a person is capable of."

Pax exchanges an uneasy glance with me and his parents.

Better find Deedie.

Before one of these Reflectives find her and she gets "cleaned."

5

Deegan

"Mitchell!" I gasp, bent over with my palms flat on my lower thighs. I glance up. "I can't. Slow down."

Mitchell shakes his head. "No. Can. Do." He turns around, casting a seething look beyond where I stand. His glittering eyes are demented sapphires in his face. "What if that dick comes after us?" He skates a hand over his short black hair, and a clump falls out.

I straighten, staring at the stranded hair in Mitchell's hand, and my exhaustion becomes despair. I burst into tears. Again.

We've already been through one "weak girl" round before. I swear I'm not one of *those girls*—the ones who can't tolerate a little stress and have to have a *man* take over. Lame. Unfortunately, I'm overloaded.

Mitchell's fingers come away from his head with black hairs clinging to a piece of scalp.

I slap my hands over my mouth. *I can't keep my zombie perfect.* I'm an AftD failure.

"Now, listen here," Mitchell begins as he walks back the two meters to where I stand, bawling my eyes out like a "big whah-baby," as Pax calls me when he's pissed at me.

Mitchell casually flicks the tuft of hair and scalp on to the ground.

I wail harder. *Can't I do anything right?*

Mitchell halts, tilts his head to the right, and cups his chin. Some of the skin sloughs away with the motion, and I hiccup a sob.

"Is this like a PMS thing?"

I stop crying and get mad instead. "PMS?" I splutter. Then I think quickly—*Is my period close?* Oh my God, is there a chance I might even have a period, *and* it would think to start in this weird-ass world? *Gah!*

Mitchell studies my morphing expressions, and his shoulders start shaking as his face breaks in a grin. A laugh bursts out of him.

My eyebrows fall like bricks above my eyes. "I'm going to kill you."

Mitchell grins—his mouth is dark, I notice with frustration—as his laughter peals out. "Already dead, sweetheart."

"Ah!" I yell, spinning in a slow circle, facing away from him. I don't want to see his rotting face right now. I fold my arms.

Mitchell puts his arms around me from behind. The smell of Mitchell and vague rot suffuse my senses, and suddenly, I want to cry again.

I bite my lip. Hard. "You didn't have to be mean."

"Don't know how to deal with the waterworks, Deegan." His strong fingers trail down my arms, and gooseflesh breaks out like a wake behind a boat.

I turn slowly in his embrace.

Mitchell is perfect and whole again.

"How?" I ask in wonder, stroking a finger down a jaw forever wearing a beard somewhere between stubble and full.

Mitchell shrugs, his big hands cupping my shoulders. "I think—and, boy, don't hold me to this because I've been a zombie for less than a week—but it's your age."

I flinch. No girl in the universe wants the guy she thinks is hot telling her she's too young. Even if he *is* dead.

He instantly reads my face, my sloppy emotions zinging through our tight bond. "No, Deegan. I mean, you're young in your *abilities*. These psychic powers or whatever? Like *X Men*."

I frown. *X Who?*

He waves away my confusion. "There were these movies in my time about a bunch of people that had paranormal abilities, and they threw everyone into a tizzy. It was good against evil. That kind of thing."

I just stare. Finally, I say, "Well, truth *is* stranger than fiction." At least, that's what Gramps always says.

Mitchell laughs, caressing my cheekbone with a cal-loused finger. "You're a crazy girl, Deegan."

I nod. "Yeah." But my voice is unhappy. I want my family. *I want Mitchell to stop rotting.*

I don't ever want to see Reflective Ryan again. That makes me think of something. "Who *was* that jerk?"

"The soldier?"

My brows draw together. I lean my head back to see him better and arch an eyebrow, leaning away from him. "How do you know he was a soldier?"

"I was a Navy Seal." Mitchell looks off into the dis-tance. A small lake lies a kilometer or so away from us. Dark evergreens stand watch over its shimmering sur-face. "When my brother and sister were... taken—" He pauses over the word. "I was on leave from the Navy. After they died, I threw myself back into another tour in Afghanistan."

I rummage my brain for late-twentieth history then hit on it, grimacing at my knowledge base. We have not had real war since that era. There have been too many more important issues. Like having enough people.

His blue eyes meet mine, and he takes hold of my hands. Mitchell shrugs. "I didn't want to live after what happened to them, Deegan. I was exonerated of all of it—my command saw fit to give me grieving time. I didn't want that. I wanted focus." He points his index and middle fingers towards his eyes, then away.

My heart pounds. I know Mitchell is going to tell me how he passed away. I don't want to hear it.

Not yet.

Every nerve is taut with listening anyway.

The anticipation of impending doom is so much like when Uncle Clyde told us his story about saving the busload of kids during the accident that caused his death that I want to cover my ears.

I raised this man in a desperate cast of the line. Mitchell came like a fish on a hook—saved me.

But I didn't catch a minnow. I caught a shark.

And Mitchell has teeth.

So I listen, because I'm responsible for him being alive again. I listen because I care. Too much.

And I think I'm falling for him. I'm too young—*and he's dead.*

But none of those facts appear to matter.

"What happened?" My hands escape his, and I wrap my fingers around part of his forearms. He's such a big guy that my fingertips don't meet.

A rough exhale shoots out of him. "We were on a mission. In and out. We used to call it 'a burger.'"

I frown, squeezing his arms in encouragement while my eyes search his face.

Mitchell sighs, his gaze returning to the far-off lake. "Used to be a burger joint called In-N-Out Burger." He gives an abrupt chuckle. "Anyway—*burger.*"

Mitchell's face takes on lines of anguish. He won't want to tell the story twice. "Easy, right?" His voice cracks.

I don't think. I just move into the circle of his arms.

He crushes me against him, his body overwhelming mine.

A heart I caused to beat thumps against my wet cheek. He strokes the back of my disheveled hair.

"We're moving into the low-tech area—farmers, kids… civilians. We've lost one of our own, need to get him back. He scouted, then we lost contact. Simple." His chin tucks against the top of my head. His Adam's apple vibrates against my forehead. "Burger," he whispers.

But I hear. I hear so much more than the words. See, because he's my zombie. And I'm his mistress. And in a really creepy kind of way, I get the melt-off from his emotions like an iceberg calving chunks of ice. *Now?* It's more like chunks of heart—broken and sliding into a miserable glacial ocean.

Never to warm again. Feel. *Live.*

I tighten my grip on his waist, feeling the muscles at his flanks as he tenses, preparing to tell me more.

"Casper was dead, of course," Mitchell recounts softly.

Of course. I suck in my breath. Hold it.

Like a ghost. I remember Gramps saying something about a ghost named Casper that was a popular show before pulse.

An ugly coincidence.

"They tortured him in such a way I know they didn't get anything outta him."

His breath warms my scalp.

I dampen his slightly scratchy wooly flannel overshirt with my sadness. "Who?"

Mitchell moves away, cradling my face, searching my eyes. "The common guy. The ones al-Qaeda uses. Expendable flesh." His chuckle is dark this time, and a shadow of who he is breathes across his features. Merciless. Unyielding. "He didn't know who he'd captured."

I see the wink of silver-toned metal against his large neck and remember the sound of a necklace from before. *Dog tags*, Gramps calls them.

His eyes bore into mine, and I swallow past the lump of fear and anxiety that's stuck in my throat.

"When we got through with him…" Mitchell pauses, and a horrible mudslide of visuals pour through my mind. "We moved on to the higher sect. Should have taken back-up. But Eddie V. and me, we wanted first dibs. We let our vengeance get in the way of our brains." His hand moves from his temple—as though pulled by an invisible string—to the spot directly over his heart.

"I guess they awarded me the Congressional Medal of Honor." Irony twists his lips. "Posthumously, of course."

Our silence is swollen. Empty. Yet full at the same time. After an entire minute has passed, he says, "Got Eddie V. out."

I bite my lip. Release. "What happened to you, Mitchell?"

"They burnt me alive." His voice is devoid of emotion.

A sound squeezes out between my lips. Raw nerves on breath. "Mitchell."

"Shhh, I only felt it a little bit, at the beginning." He pulls away, a smile softening the line of his lips.

I choke back tears.

Then a river of water pours out of my eyes, and Mitchell brushes what he can from my cheeks.

"Deegan." He leans forward and presses a kiss to my forehead.

My body quivers with my anger. "I hate that they hurt you."

He leans away. "If they hadn't killed me, I wouldn't have found you. But I do have a very important question."

His eyebrows sweep up, and I laugh. It's an inappropriate response, but everything was so serious, then he does this *face.*

"Is my death funny?" Mitchell puts his palm to his chest, mock-insulted.

God no. I shake my head vigorously, giggles turning to gales.

"Nice, Deegan. Yuk it up. *So* compassionate."

I try to defend my stupidity and can't. Planting my hands on my knees, I take big whoops of air. My chin rises, and I meet his solemn eyes.

"Better?" he asks.

I nod. "Yeah. But I—you didn't need to tell me that." Straightening, I gnaw at my lip again. After a few seconds of searching his face, I see a question in the arrangement of his features. "So ask."

He dips his chin. "How, with the way I died, can I look like this again? All perfect."

I shake my head, and small hairs float into my face from the long mess of my braid. "I don't know. If my dad was here, he'd know." I hate saying the next part, but it might make more sense if I do. "Did they-they…" I stammer. "Burn all of you?" I whisper that last.

He remains unfazed. "No. They cooked me enough to kill me, but parts of me weren't touched. I remember." He gives the top of his skull a light tap.

I look sharply at him. "Your head?"

He raps on his skull. "Hard-headed, though they tried their damnedest."

I get excited. "That might be it. No AftD can raise anyone if they don't have brains."

"Yummy," Mitchell says instantly.

I roll my eyes.

"What?" his gaze narrows on me.

"Are you telling me you like brains?"

Mitchell snorts as though my question is ridiculous. "Absolutely."

Zombies. I grin.

He grins back. "Yeah, if that chump Ryan had stuck around long enough, might have gotten after him." He waggles his brows.

I make a fake gag noise. "Gross!"

"No worries. All those crows were working him over. Have a lot of love for that." His grin widens. He's obviously thinking about the possibility of Ryan getting pecked to death.

I shiver.

"Speaking of that guy…" Mitchell paces away from me.

The sun is still high over our heads.

I'm gauging the time of day to be sometime early afternoon. But who knows? I guess Dad would, since he's the only one on the planet who wears a wristwatch. A winder, too.

He snickers. "If he lives through peck heaven"— Mitchell jerks his thumb back from the direction we just ran from—"he might want a little payback."

I shift wide eyes to his, my chest tightening like a vice.

His gaze sharpens on my features—my fear. "Don't be afraid, Deegan."

"I am," I admit immediately. "He said something about how he was born the way he was and my 'Atomic' ability can't zap him." My lip trembles with the need to break down again, but I can't be a baby every time the wind blows. Only sometimes. My lips quirk instead of pout. I take deep breaths, attempting to settle my feelings.

"Wait. What?" His face hardens. "Atomic? *Zap*?" Then realization lights his face. "Right. Your black hole thing?"

Yeah, my black hole thingie. That little nothing I can do. *That.*

I sigh. "Yes. I tried to get him off me, get rid of him." I cast my eyes to the ground, noting my All Stars sneakers are toast. "Even though I'm not supposed to—"

"Hey!" Mitchell stands before me again. "Survival of the fittest, right?" He winks.

I pierce him with an intense look, my brows meeting. "Gramps always says that." Because it's true.

He chuckles, bending down to give me a quick kiss on my cheek. "Smart dude."

I nod. His comment makes me miss my family all over again.

We're silent for a few seconds.

"I knew Ryan was a soldier because of the way he handled himself. I'm damn glad I can't feel pain—and that I'm stronger than fuck." He slides a guilty glance my way.

"Forget it." I laugh softly. "My brother's got the worst trash mouth on the planet."

"And a big chip on his shoulder."

I bristle at that a little, though it's the absolute truth. "He's got a lot to deal with."

"Uh-huh."

I look quickly at Mitchell. "I'm sorry. I didn't mean you haven't—didn't." *God, I'm so dumb.* Technically, I'm not. But when I'm around Mitchell, my IQ seems to drop about fifty points.

"It's okay," he says softly. "Your bro? He seems okay, just protective. But he's a hothead. I'd know the type a hundred miles off."

"Miles?" I ask with a lilt. My eyes are probably twinkling at him.

Mitchell crosses his arms, expression speculative. "What do *you* say?"

"Kilometers."

"Damn," he says, lips tweaking. "They finally went metric." He gives a small shake of his head.

"Yeah, a million years ago."

His look is bittersweet. "Yeah," he answers softly, almost to himself.

I grab his hand, and he squeezes mine back. "Ryan will come after us. If he survives 'The Pecking,' he'll come."

"Yes," I concede, a vague smile planted on my lips. Ryan seemed pretty determined. "He says this world doesn't allow Death Bringers and Atomics."

"Death Bringer. That's cute." The corners of his lips curve.

I smirk. "Not *really*. In fact, it's made me the most ineligible senior ever to grace the United States."

"You're a senior?" Mitchell drops my hand. "In high school?"

A blush heats my face, and I can only hope that my dusky skin doesn't show it. Truth time. "Actually, I skipped a grade."

Mitchell backs up another step. "I kissed you." His voice is pancake flat.

I wince. "Yeah, but—"

Mitchell shakes his head. "No. I don't think so, Deegan. I'm not—I was nearly twenty-one when I was killed. I'm not going after some schoolgirl."

God! "It's not like that."

He glares at me. "What's it like then?"

Fine. "I'm of age. In this time, sixteen is the age of automatic emancipation."

"Are you just telling me that?"

My face bursts into flames. "No," I say in harsh reply, tossing razor blades with my eyes.

"Fine." He draws out the word. "But in my time, any girl under eighteen was off limits."

I fold my arms under my breasts, and his eyes dilate. *Hmm.* "You didn't seem to be too concerned about that when we were macking earlier!"

I stomp off toward the lake, not caring about where Reflective Ryan might be skulking, my family, or anything. It's all about The Feels.

And mine are pretty pissed off right about now.

Mitchell crashes right after, and I ignore him. He spins me around, gripping my shoulders. "Listen to me, and listen good. You're not some chick to bang and release like a fucking fish, Deegan."

My eyes widen to bulging at his words. My breath is wedged in my throat like a bloated thorn.

"You're this wonderful, thrilling, life-altering—" He snorts before plowing forward with his diatribe. "*Great* girl, who's almost a woman, and I'm *not* going to queer that by being selfish."

I look up into his eyes, the most gorgeous blue I've ever beheld, a cerulean ocean without end.

His grip is tight, not bruising like the one Ryan had me in.

My teeth don't rattle in Mitchell's hands; they ache along with my heart, my body.

I lift my hands, and like a starving man, he watches them come.

When I reach his face, I cradle his jaw. The short hairs of his beard tickle the skin of my palms.

"Be selfish," I whisper. "Be very, very selfish."

Then I'm rising on my tiptoes and pressing my lips to his.

Mitchell resists.

My lips move, molding to his, pecking and dipping.

"Dee—"

My tongue plunges inside his mouth as I wrap my arms around his thick neck.

Mitchell groans, jerking me against him and carding his fingers through my hair.

Selfish has a name now.

Love.

6

Pax

"What are you called in your world?" Jasper asks, small hands knotted behind her back.

I flick a sidelong glance at her. Good thing Beth Jasper handed me my ass—confirming I'm still a Body in this world. It's not that she's strong and big. She's skilled.

It was uncanny as fuck that Jasper seemed to anticipate my every move. Of course, I thought I'd just *subdue* her. Gramps says assuming makes an ass out of you—and me.

Yeah, that was about it.

I didn't want to hurt a girl, even if the chick brought it. Then it became just about surviving her.

Now Jasper studies me as she propels her body forward. Her movements are timed, smooth. There's a smoldering grace to her gait; Merrick steps gamely beside her with that same perfect rhythm.

She frowns, clearly growing impatient without an answer.

Merrick scowls, his body tense.

Answering's good. "I—well, there used to be these people called Dimensionals on my Earth."

Jasper nods, waiting for me to continue.

Sure taking the news about world flippers well. I suck a rough inhale then let it out. "Anyways, there aren't any more Dimensionals. And *my* ability is uncatalogued."

"Let's not spill our guts, Pax," Gramps says, cagey style coming onpulse.

I smile. *He never trusts.* Never. "I think it's okay, Gramps. They're like me."

"Remember where we started from," Dad comments, eyeing the two Reflectives.

Merrick sends a sharp look Dad's way. "We were responding to *your* force. Our directives disallow harming you unless you engage us first."

Jasper sighs and recites, "The sixth: Take life only in defense of another."

Merrick gives a curt nod of agreement, and a look passes between the two.

Strange rangers, these guys. "Okay, *yeah*. What I was saying is—I can go to parallel dimensions."

Jasper and Merrick stop walking; the town is just below us. This close, I can make out that a boatload of

Roman-looking architecture. Marble with apricot vein-
ing glitters like sherbet in cream.

Dad, Mom, Uncle John, Tiff, Jonesy, and Sophie
bring up the rear. Gramps is beside me.

The horde follows at a safe distance. I'm not sure
what to do about them, and Jonesy seems unbothered.
As usual.

"You say that you travel to the thirteen sectors?"

Hell, it's like infinity sectors. I frown. "My family
calls it *blinking*."

"Show us," Merrick commands.

"Is this where I roll over, play dead, and get my ass
patted like a good dog?"

Dad groans, and Gramps snorts.

I shrug. "Come on, Dad." *Merrick's a cockbite.* Plain
and simple.

Merrick's hands fist.

"Jeb," Jasper says in a low voice, and her hand touches
his forearm lightly, "he's a youngling."

See? Cock. Bite. And what's the youngling bullshittery?
Merrick grits his teeth.

"I will switch to your diction," Jasper says, one eye
on her partner.

My what?

"What does your government call people who can
Reflect?"

Instantly, the formal speech drops, and she sounds
like she's from my hometown. Not a fan. "I don't know

what this 'reflect' thing is, but I don't need glass or mirrors or whatever. And I don't know about the thirteen world thing. I can move"—my palm swings to the left than right between the two Reflectives and me—"into many worlds." I hold my pointer finger and thumb barely apart, trying to show them the space between worlds is as thin as a pane of glass.

Merrick's jaw locks. "He is *not* Reflective."

I've been trying to say. This guy's like a funeral director. Fucking humorless. I cross my arms, rocking back on my heels.

"How many worlds?" Jasper asks in a slightly awe-struck voice.

I hesitate, not sure if my answer will be braggy or what.

"Go ahead, Pax," Mom says in her ultra-encouraging voice.

I smirk. *Here goes.* "All of them." A heavy dose of *duh* is in my answer.

The Reflectives exchange a glance so full, I can't decipher it. "What?"

They step closer. "You are dangerous, Pax of Three," Merrick comments.

I retreat the step they gained. "That's why I'm not alerting the media back in my world, guys."

"Can you do this *blinking* here?"

I jerk my chin back. "Yeah."

Jasper puts her hand on Merrick's arm again, taking the verbal reins. "Would you demonstrate?"

I shake my head. "I don't have enough practice. I screwed up, couldn't get anyone to a specific place if I tried."

"Not true, dude. You got us to psycho-bot world twice." Jonesy grins. The zombies crowd him. "Hey, Team Dead, back off. Ya smell like bad ground beef."

God. Jonesy makes a shitty AftD.

And going to bot world worked out so well. Of course, the bot world *did* cure Gram's cancer. Trying to look for the good shit in this mess. Not seeing it.

"Psycho-bot world?" Merrick's brows draw together.

He's a fucking downer. "Yeah. Cyborg's and shit. Only Organics allowed."

Merrick's jaw slides back and forth.

"Healers?" Jasper asks, clearly puzzled.

I nod. "Yeah, same thing as Organics. But these bot things tried to kill us on sight."

Murmurs of assent spring up around me.

"I do not know this world."

Jasper looks to Merrick. "If he is a parallel… Reflective—"

Merrick opens his mouth.

Jasper swings a warding palm between them before finishing her thought. "Of sorts, then he is a Three native…"

Merrick picks up her train of thinking. "And would instinctively shift to parallels of his own world."

An exhale eases out of Jasper, and she nods once. "Yes."

"So what?" I ask. *This is so not important.* I want to get the hell out of Reflect-o world, escape the crazy-ass Parker, and find Dee. That's all the shits I give.

"What is it?" Jasper asks Merrick, and we stare at him.

"From my experience on the other sectors, there are abilities that will not drop, no matter where the humanoid travels."

"Huh?" I pinch the bridge of my nose and pace away, hiding my expression.

Dad sees it and sighs, drawing Mom close.

"What he's saying is"—she surveys our group, eyes narrowing on the rotting zombies—"is that there are primary abilities. There's a short list."

Now she's speaking my language.

"There's the rare Atomic, as well as a Parallel and three others. No matter where said humanoid would go, those abilities would remain innate."

I shoot my parents a loaded glance when Jasper says *Atomic.* Kinda like she said *bomb.* That's all we need is Dee in the eye of this shitstorm.

Uncle John asks, "Humanoid?"

Nice. *Like turkeys who talk or what?*

Merrick hikes his chin. "There are many other species who assume a basic humanoid body but do not fall strictly within human norms."

Okay.

"Don't care too much," Jonesy comments, hiking his chin at the nearest zombie. His eyeball sort of plops out, falling into the grass with a stealthy rustling sound.

Uncle John slaps his forehead.

Jonesy glares. "Hey, Terran, cool your jets, man. Just trying to figure a way outta here."

Uncle John glances at the dozen corpses busy melting like human gore candles and silently dies of embarrassment.

"Not without Deegan, Jonesy," Mom says, sounding vaguely insulted.

"Deegan?" the Reflectives chime together.

Tiff cracks another loud bubble, mumbling something that sounds suspiciously like "twins."

Merrick levels a hard glance at her.

She grins. "Don't get intimidated easily. And I'm as sober as I've never wanted to be, so there's that."

John dips his chin, practicing deep breathing and looking at the ground.

I figured adulting would be easier. Seems like my parents' friends are having a helluva time.

"Deegan's my sister. Dee." A tight knot forms in my chest.

"*Ah.*" Jasper kicks her chin up. "Why is she not with you?"

Good question. Because I dropped her during a *blink*. Like some of the others. Maybe that big mouthbreather Mitchell is still with her. He goes hard; he won't let anything happen.

I hope. The knot in my chest tightens unbearably.

"Is she a youngling, as well?" Merrick asks.

"I'm a man," I correct.

Merrick's slow burning perusal sweeps from my head to my toes. "You have the body of a man and the mouth of a boy. Youngling."

Gramps makes a noise, and I pivot, staring at him.

"Sorry, son. He has a way with words."

Yeah, a shitty one. "She's younger than me."

"What is her gift?" Jasper asks.

What is her ability? I translate.

"No, Pax," Mom cautions.

Like I'd fucking tell these two sector assassins that my sister is an Atomic. Black hole queen. Space and continuum disruptor extraordinaire.

Then Dee shows up and takes all the guess work out of everything, along with her zombie and a Reflective like a partridge in a pear tree. But this guy is serial killer bad, and his sights are on my sister.

Bad call.

7

Gramps

Oh hell.

There's Deedie and her friendly zombie—and one of those Reflective people.

My eyes do the initial sweep of the guy. *What in the blue hell is all that over his face?* It looks like chunks of his skin are missing, and dime-sized pieces of bone gleam in the fading afternoon light, giving him a mottled appearance.

Something got after that fella—good.

Deedie yelps when he snaps into our presence with that curly-cue iridescent whip of glitter the other two Reflectives employed.

I expect unicorns to crop up any moment and start pissing rainbows. I snort, loving the visual.

"Oops," Pax says, and my face swivels to him. His expression is sheepish.

"Delayed *blink*?" he comments.

Caleb and Jade simultaneously put their hands to their heads like a whopper of a headache might be coming on.

My eyeballs shoot upward like rockets. *Dear God.*

The new Reflective, whoever he is, turns to the other two. "Merrick. Jasper." His lips curl when he says the woman's name, and I can tell there's no love lost there.

The new guy's uniform matches the woman's, but Merrick's is slightly different. More permanent, if I was to take a wag.

"Inductee Ryan," Merrick says, and his hands loosen from their knotted perch at his back.

Ryan glares at Merrick.

Jasper gives a disdainful teeth-baring smile. "Ryan."

Small tells. Only someone with my background would notice that these three are on uneasy terms, at best.

At worst? *We'll see.*

Deedie's big zombie glowers at Ryan, moving in front of her protectively.

Ah.

That says a lot. It's been my experience that zombies are purists. Mitch doesn't like Ryan. And that means he has a reason not to.

Good enough for me. Immediately, I go on the defensive. Not a stretch.

The two Reflectives notice the wounds on Ryan's face as his attention moves to Jonesy's hastily animated horde.

Didn't his wounds look worse when he first appeared on the scene?

"Report," Merrick commands Ryan.

The younger man doesn't like it. His lip lifts like he's a pit bull in the ring.

Nice camaraderie with this group.

"It's her, this Three." He points an accusing finger at Deedie.

Mitch hisses.

This is rich.

"Deegan, what's going on?" Caleb asks.

Deedie looks from her dad to Ryan. Fearfully. Now Deedie isn't the most assertive little girl, but when she gets her dander up, she handles most things fine.

I frown, thinking of the missing hands of some of the new Graysheet types. *Maybe there's room for improvement.*

Merrick and Jasper look at Deedie then Mitch.

Jasper's eyes widen. "Reanimated human." She lumps in Mitch with Jonesy's mess, her eyes shifting between Deedie's zombie and the dozen rot-boys flanking Jones.

Doesn't seem fair. Mitch looks a helluva lot better than Jonesy's undead troops.

"Yes," Merrick comments in a voice so neutral, I understand instinctively the man's unflappability is failing.

"She is a Death Bringer, Merrick—and, an Atomic."

Their gazes narrow on Deedie.

I move forward, and they turn to me. Actually, Jasper turns toward me, and Merrick faces everyone else.

Their posture is utterly different. Tense. Resolute.

Fuck a duck. "Hold on," I say quickly, "let's not do anything rash."

"Put a lid on it, old man," Ryan says without glancing in my direction. His words are clipped and dismissive.

Rude twerp. And for the record, I loathe his use of our language.

Merrick frowns. "How did you get those wounds on your person?" He directs the question at Ryan, but his eyes are on Deedie.

"Crows." He jerks his chin toward Deedie. "The little bitch Death Bringer summoned them."

Mitch growls. *Liking him more all the time. Yessiree.*

"I do not appreciate your tone, hooligan." This is from our man, Clyde.

Now *he* is someone I see eye-to-eye with. I grunt. Good to have him on the team. Very few words, but lots of action. Unfortunately, Clyde seems to be outgunned as it were. Similarly, Caleb sets everything on fire but doesn't seem to be AftD—that kind of thing is happening in spades here.

Ryan's feet burst into flames, and he leaps like he was goosed in the ass.

Excellent. Sometimes timing just works.

"Nice, Dad." Pax smirks.

Jonesy pushes up his sunglasses, and they come apart, falling from the bridge of his nose.

He bends to retrieve them.

Pesky metal screws. Metal does weird shit when one travels the Paxton Blinking Highway.

Ryan shouts what sounds like a swearword in the Reflective language, then he vanishes. A burst of serpentine glittering light flashing before his form slams into the lens that had just been covering Jonesy's right eyeball.

"Shee-*it*!" Jonesy shrieks, jumping back.

His zombies tense.

Ryan reappears before Deedie.

I react before I can stop myself—damn near a life-long trend. A hard thought has me moving through Ryan before his form completely solidifies.

Well isn't this nifty?

I figure I've got less than a second until he takes me, so I don't stand around being introspective. I jack my fist into that soft spot under his jaw, and Ryan stumbles backward, trying to reclaim some oxygen.

Ryan's hop to my great-granddaughter seemed to put out his fire.

I look at Caleb and cock an eyebrow.

Jonesy steps on what remains of his sunglasses with a "fuck that" followed by a crunching noise.

"Mac!"

I duck, and a hand passes through where my head would have been. Jerking my ceramic work knife out of my pants, I flick the blade and hammer it in Ryan's kneecap.

He howls, and I punch the hilt, breaking the blade off inside his leg.

That'll put a pause in your step.

He moves, and I throw myself backward. My bag of tricks is about empty when Pax and Mitch move in.

"Stop, or we will kill you."

My gaze shifts to Merrick. "What about all your fancy-smancy directives?" I nod knowingly. "This pain in our ass is gunning for Deedie, and we aren't going to sit around while he *cleans* her."

I harrumph, and he and Jasper move toward Ryan as Mitch and Pax each grab an arm.

The little girl that kicked my old ass disappears. She is much smoother than Ryan.

Her tailwind sinks into the crushed glass of Jonesy's ruined lenses. The remnants are no greater than a pea.

And she's suddenly in front of the guys holding Ryan.

"Jasper!" Merrick hollers and runs toward her. She sucker punches Pax, and he folds.

Hard charger. Gotta admire the little filly. But Mitch. *Ah*—Mitch, *a zombie after my own heart.*

Jasper's fist sinks, and he grabs her wrist.

She yanks, and he pulls.

"Sorry," he says. Then he picks her up and throws her about twenty feet from their position.

Ryan punches Mitch, and the skin of his chin sloughs off with the blow.

Oh my.

Deedie starts bawling.

Not great timing, I have to admit.

Clyde comes to stand beside me. "What to do?"

I nod. It's a conundrum. "Pax!" I holler.

Merrick turns, and Pax sits up straight and kicks the man's kneecap. He winces.

And by God, I know that hurt like a sonofabitch.

Pax stands, and Merrick slaps him.

The Reflectives are as tough as nails, and Pax yelps as his face rocks back. But he latches on to Merrick.

Shadows of the coming night slide across the grass, and Merrick's eyes widen. They darken like cups of soft black in his face.

Pax's eyes tighten, then he *blinks.* His bluish-gray eyes, so like Ali's, move like blackened turquoise under a sheet of opaque ice. The thin membrane of his second eyelid floats over the color, muting it.

Instantly, worlds appear like sheets of glass covered by water.

Holy mother of God. It's like being in the funhouse full of reflections without end.

There are a million Macs. I see variations of my face, one after another after another. My next swallow is painful, my next breath, shallow.

Not losing my shit, I tell myself like a command.

"Not this again," Tiff mutters, joining hands with whoever is beside her.

Merrick resists.

"Holy fucking cow, Pax's *blinking* trumps mirror hopping!" Jonesy chortles. He spares a quick glance for the horde and shrugs. "Sorry, Dead Dudes."

"Not now, Jones," John Terran says in a flat voice.

Jonesy grunts dismissively. "Chill, Terran."

Sophie grabs Jonesy's hand, and everyone holds on.

Pax *blinks* again, and we travel to wherever my great-grandson decides to take us.

I can hope for my place.

It's like this: hope in one hand and shit in the other and see which one fills up faster.

Guess where wishing got me?

Back in the land 'o bots.

Marvelous.

8

Deegan

Our kiss is crushed by heat.
I know that heat.

It's not the newfound passion with my zombie; it's *blinking*. But Pax isn't here—so how are we moving?

One second, I'm pressed up against my zombie, sharing a kiss I know would ground me for life, and the next second, we're landing in a pile of entangled limbs.

I yelp at the landing. My arm's twisted behind me by Mitchell's hold. He rearranges me so I'm not pinned, and I sit upright.

The smell of rot hits me first. Alarming to some, it's nothing to me. The scent is *eau de zombie*.

Badly raised zombies.

I rub my eyes, nausea gripping and releasing me from the shift from one place to another. The sensation when

Pax *blinks* from area to area within the same world is like when a rollercoaster first lurches on the rails and my stomach does a toss as I hurtle down the slope.

Mitchell grips me by my waist and easily heaves me to standing. His grip is firm, as though he knows I'm about ready to puke.

I quickly take in the scene then gasp.

Ryan is here—missing chunks of flesh that reveal wounds that glow slightly. His bone shows through gouged skin.

"Oh, my god," I whisper.

"The Pecking," Mitchell comments noncommittally.

Ryan swings his face to us, and Mitchell takes a step back with me in his arms. He hisses.

Ryan points at us, and I belatedly notice his feet are smoldering. I shift my eyes to Dad, and he's smirking. *Huh.* The soldier Reflective guy's a mess.

"Pax," I say without turning, a quiver in my voice.

"Dee, now's not a hot time to chat."

Right, but now's a good time to *get away*.

I can feel who raised the horde about four meters from where Mitchell and I stand.

My eyes flick to Jonesy.

That's bad. Zombies are so much an extension of the raiser. And apparently, on this world, Jonesy is AftD.

As though on cue, Jonesy slaps one of his zombies on the back and says, "Hey, guys, take care of this dude." His dark eyebrows quirk, and he jerks his chin toward Ryan.

The zombies' eyes (those who have eyeballs) fall on Ryan. *Can't think of a better guy to get the evil zombie eye.* I shudder, thinking about my time in the cell when he was talking about doing me because I'm Atomic.

The dead begin to shamble toward Ryan.

Ryan points again, with one eye on the ever-present undead crew. "She is a Death Bringer and an Atomic!" he announces triumphantly.

The man, who I remember popping up before, says, "She will need to be brought before council."

No.

Pax gives me a tense sideways look as the tight rotting horde moves closer to Ryan. He spares them a glance of pure distaste. If it hadn't been happening to me, I would think it was funny. As it is, nothing about this world is remotely humorous.

The first zombie touches Ryan's uniform, leaving a slug trail of rotting gore.

Ryan smacks the zombie's wrist, and its hand falls off.

Gah. I rub my sweaty palms on my jeans.

The hand falls to the ground, twitches, and begins its slow journey back to Ryan.

"Righteous!" Jonesy shouts with a whoop. I'm so glad someone is enjoying himself.

Aunt Tiff snaps a bubble that makes everyone who's living startle.

"He manhandled me!" I yell at the other two Reflectives over the din of zombies getting beat up by Ryan.

I notice the two others (one is a girl) are not really helping. *Like zombies aren't a threat.* So not true.

Then I notice the snakes.

I jerk my chin in the direction of the death signature I can feel like a high-frequency thread of noise.

Tiff. She smirks, crossing her skinny arms underneath her boobs. "Gotta love the dead."

The snakes sidewind toward Ryan.

The other Reflective guy's sharp gaze finds the snakes in the grass. Literally.

I laugh and notice I only have a slight edge of hysteria. Mitchell takes my hand. I breathe deeply.

"Jasper," the other guy Reflective says in a voice so neutral, it's colorless. The girl, small and dark like me, turns to him.

"Merrick, she's summoned the reptiles."

They've got it wrong. They can't read death signatures.

I look to Dad, and I peg him as a one-point. Tiff is four plus, and I feel excellent—flexing my AftD muscle. The energy inside me swells, and more dead come. A tremble flows through Jonesy's horde.

Jonesy's head whips in my direction, a frown marring the space between his eyes. "No, sister, don't mess with Team Rot. They're on a mission."

I nod, in a sort of trance. Vaguely, I hear Mom and Dad exchanging heated words.

Then Sophie, John, Tiff, and Uncle Clyde smack hands, and I know what will happen.

Pax will *blink* us.

My power beats inside me, unsatisfied.

"Deegan, pull it back," Mitchell says.

Feels good to use the power.

He turns me, and we face each other.

Small scrapes and abrasions caused by the rapid inner-world shift smooth on his face as I watch, repaired by the overflow of my death energy.

"Death Bringer," the female says in a commanding strike of two words.

I turn toward her, my head moving as though I'm underwater, and I catch sight of the dead animals I've unwittingly called from the surrounding forest.

The lake we'd been so close to earlier, before Pax *blinked* us to this new location, is now far away.

Her dark eyes find mine, so deep brown that the pupils hide in the irises. "Do not use this power in Papilio."

Fine. I tilt my head. "Call off Ryan."

Jasper turns to Ryan. "Stop this."

Merrick gives a curt nod in clear agreement. "This is not the way of it, Ryan."

Ryan bares his teeth, and my power flares in response. Every dead animal within a kilometer moves toward Ryan. Black eyes hold his death in their gazes.

Ryan shoves another zombie to the ground, where it falls to its butt and rolls out of the fall before clumsily shuffling to a stand to come at Ryan again. "The council need never know. Cleanse her now. This Three is everything that is dangerous."

Someone grabs my hand, and Mitchell is latched on to me like a barnacle. I feel Pax's power flow through me like a flog of fire.

Jonesy says, "Sorry, Dead Dudes."

Heat rushes up my neck, suffusing my head. The Reflective pair sharpen their gazes on me while the dead animals and zombies converge.

My last clear image is of Ryan tearing the limb off one of the zombies then using the ball joint of the socket to bludgeon its head.

Brains explode in a shower of skull shards and gray matter. The head breaks from the spinal cord and rolls to Ryan's feet. The zombie's mouth opens and tries to take off the toe of his boot with the few teeth that remain.

Then Ryan's image wavers. The horde looks as though they're melting. Or like I'm seeing the Reflectives and the undead behind water that skates over glass.

Then we're gone.

Pax has *blinked*, and the fire and ice march across my skin like ants on the hills and valleys of my body.

When we roll out of Papilio into the new world, I want to cry. Before Mitchell even confirms where we are—I know.

I don't want to be in bot world.

And of course, that's where we land.

I don't throw up, but I'm on my hands and knees doing a version of the quick swallows. If you're the *blinker*, I guess everything's A-Okay. In my case, my blinking at nighttime only enhances my vision by about a billion, but still—it's not me traveling to parallel dimensions. I'm just the rider, and I feel terrible.

"Deedie?"

I swing my head in the direction of Gramps's voice. "Yeah, Gramps," I manage a hushed whisper.

"Gonna need to get up. We need your paranormal mojo on board."

On board for what? I hear a bot scream, and that answers the question.

I gulp back my gorge, my fear. "Move," I say without enthusiasm, and Gramps scoots to the left.

A bot—cyborg—whatever the thing is, has sighted us and opened its mouth for round two. A cavernous mechanical hole in its smooth face yawns black, and I briefly think of zombies then make sure none of our group's in the way.

Please God, I pray silently.

I aim my zapping ability right at the source of the noise, and the head disappears with a low crackle like gunfire heard from a great distance.

The dismantled bot drops like a sack of discarded tools.

"Damn, that is *fine*." Jonesy chuckles.

I fight tears as I cover my face with my hands.

"Sorry, pumpkin, but those pesky bots bring their friends, and we could have a challenging situation on our hands." Gramps awkwardly pats my back.

Challenging situation. My fingers split, and I look between them.

Sophie and Jonesy are bickering quietly. Dad, Mom, Aunt Tiff, and Uncle John seem to be scheming by a copse of trees.

Clyde and Mitchell stand together, their backs to me and, I instantly understand they're on guard.

I don't see Bry or Lewis. I frown. *What happened to them?* I redirect my attention to the now-silent bot.

The body parts gleam dimly in this world's late afternoon.

We got lucky on the *blinked* location. There is a stand of sparse woodland between us and what appears to be a main road.

"Need a good cry, Deedie?" Gramps asks.

I scowl at him.

He chuckles. "Is this a bad time, like girl time?" Gramps is trying for sensitive and coming off lame.

Not again. "Gramps!" I huff, jerking to my feet.

"That's better." He gives me a light thump on my head.

Maybe my period *is* going to start? Seems like every guy on whatever planet we go to needs to get a two-by-four between the eyes.

I dust off my pants and glare at Gramps. At least the tears are held at bay, and I don't want to puke anymore.

He tosses his calloused palms up in the air. "Listen, Deedie, we needed you to take care of the bot, and I was closest. We can't have it doing an *Invasion of the Body Snatchers* call-out." His dark eyebrows, now peppered with gray, shoot up.

Oh that's reasonable. Reference cinema as an analogy for this creepy-ass world.

I grunt, scanning the environment for my brother. Where the hell is Pax?

Right here.

I turn at the sound of his voice inside my skull, and he stands about two meters away.

My vision blurs, and he strides to me. "Paxton," I cry out in relief.

My brother wraps me in his arms. "I didn't know what was happening; I was so scared," I whisper against his black T-shirt.

Pax leans back, pushing a single strand of hair off my forehead as he cups the back of my head. His slate-gray-blue eyes are soft when they look at me. "Nah. Like I'd ever let anything happen to you, Dee." He swipes my tears away with his thumbs and jerks his eyebrows up. "Did you feel my cool *blink*?"

I nod, suppressing an eye roll. "How'd you *blink* me remote?"

Pax shakes his head. His longish hair swings in his eyes, and he flips it back. "Don't know. Felt you. Wanted the group together. Or some part of my subconscious was working toward it." He locks his fingers together then lets them drop. His gaze finds Mitchell.

He's already watching us with narrow eyes, while Uncle Clyde continues to restlessly survey the perimeter.

I study Pax's and Mitchell's expressions. *Why can't my brother and my hot zombie get along?*

Probably *because* my brother knows I think my zombie is hot.

I sigh. "Bot world?" I ask, trying to keep the irritation out of my voice.

Pax lifts a shoulder. "You zapped Bot Face back there." He yanks a thumb at the bot pile behind us.

I cast my eyes at my ruined All Stars as I shift my weight. "Yeah."

"Hey," Pax props my chin up with a finger. "Fuck the bots. They're not even alive."

"I love it," Jonesy says, walking up to us. "What's so cool is there's just a bot head, flying around somewhere in parts unknown." He snorts, making a twirling motion with his finger. "It's beyond cool, and if you two morose Harts can't see the humor, God help ya."

Gramps grunts.

Pax and me give Gramps the look, and his grin just gets broader.

"It's not that they *can't* see the humor. It's that everyone in our world is having ten kinds of cows because there was illegal dead people." Sophie taps her foot. She's wearing the dumbest footwear on any planet.

I don't know if I can handle all my parents' friends in one spot.

Mitchell and Uncle Clyde walk over. I sense Mitchell is at one hundred percent.

Mitchell places a possessive hand on my nape. Pax glares at the gesture, but Mitchell doesn't take his hand away.

"'Kay Dee. Time to put lover-boy back to rest. Home world. Home dirt."

Mitchell shakes his head. "Nope. Not leaving Deegan."

Paxton steps closer.

Lovely. I'm the meat in the testosterone sandwich.

"I got this, Mitch." Pax's lips twist.

"You got lucky, Paxton. You managed to *blink* Deegan out of that Reflective world and then *blink* us all back to my world." Mitchell looks around them and at the vague outline of a town that looks suspiciously like the Kent of our hometown. "But this is *not* the place where I died. This is another time. A future I was never a part of."

Pax crosses his arms, so close to me that I feel the heat of his body. His anger.

"Not my problem." Pax's eyes flick to mine. "Deegan, no offense. Dee"—his gaze sweeps back to Mitchell's—"doesn't have great control. When Brad Thompson pulled his moves—hell when she felt endangered, Dee put out the call. Could've been any handy corpse who responded. She's a four-point."

"I don't know what that means. Points? Whatever"—
Mitchell waves his hand in Pax's face, and I know the
motion is like the red blanket in front of the bull—"the
point is, *Pax...*" He pauses, those blue eyes like chips of
ice that nail my brother. "She called *me*—it could have
been anyone, like ya said. But it wasn't. And now I'm
here, and I'm not going anywhere until Deegan is safe."

"*I* can make you go to rest," Pax says in a low voice
full of promise.

Pax is AftD in this world. I put my hand on his arm.
The skin feels like stone-covered flesh. "No, Pax."

Dad and Mom walk up. "What's going on?" Dad
asks, looking at the three of us.

"Deedie's got a crush on Mitch here, and Pax has
taken exception to it." Gramps jerks up his trousers and
smooths a palm over his salt-and-pepper flat top.

I close my eyes. Outed by my great-grandpa. *Is there
a rock I can crawl under?*

"We don't have time for this," Mom says.

Time for what? My crush? This planet? Talking?
Gah! Then the impossible happens.

My period starts—in the middle of bot-world chaos
and in front of my zombie I'm crushing on.

I burst into tears, and every man moves away like I
announced I have leprosy.

Mom glares at everyone and moves in to hug me.

9

Paxton

*D*ee, what's going on?
My period just started.
What? Like right now?
Yeah.
Holy crow! Timing is dumb.
Yeah.
Okay, we'll figure this out.

Mom is hugging Dee. She latches on to her arm, and her face changes as she reads what's happening. "Oh Jesus, Deegan."

If my mom is using the guy on the cross's name, things have gone to shit.

"What's the trouble?" Gramps asks.

Dee cries harder.

Mitch tries to touch her, and she jerks away. I like that part. Not gonna lie. Prick.

He stares daggers at me. Old Mitch knows I've got the lowdown on what's bugging Dee, and he's in the dark.

Special sauce, that. "Dee's got her cycle, and we're gonna have to figure that out," I announce calmly.

"Pax!" she screams at me.

Mitchell's face puckers. He looks at Dee.

Her face couldn't be more red.

Mom says, "Paxton Sebastian Hart, you could have handled that a *lot* better."

I shrug. It's 2049. Guys sure as shit know that girls bleed once a month—and walk around doing it. Amazing.

And not so many women in my home world. It's not a bad thing—having a cycle.

"Way to go, ya tool," Mitch says.

I whirl toward Dee's zombie. "Listen, Mitch. It's not a damn secret. She's a girl. We didn't plan to jump. It's not 2010 anymore, where no one talked about shit."

Dee sits on her butt and crosses her legs.

"You're a dick," Sophie says as she walks by and punches me in the arm for emphasis.

What in the fuck is the hang up?

Dad glowers at me. "She might just be your little sister, Pax, but she counts on you to have her back."

How do I *not* have her back? I mean—fuck! We have to get Dee corks or something so she doesn't bleed out. Practicality, guys.

I stomp toward where I know the medical clinic is. They'll have menstrual cleansers there. Let's face it—no matter what world we're on, chicks bleed. If they're lucky enough.

Holy fuck. An epiphany forms. I whirl, searching for the one face I want to see.

Tiff faces me, and I don't have telepathy, but I can read her expression, despite her tears.

"Pax," she breathes.

I know. My heartbeat climbs into my throat, and *I know.* "You're on the rag?" I ask hopefully, my eyes jumping around her features.

Then Uncle John punches me, and I go down hard.

"Good job," Mitch says in the background.

Dick.

"No!" Tiff bellows, throwing herself beside me where I lay flat on my back.

I blink. And no, it's not changing worlds, guys. Stars wink on and off in my vision.

Terran's wild hair stands up in auburn tufts, and his pale-blue eyes are hard flints of angry sky as they gaze down at me.

"Fertile," I croak through a rapidly swelling mouth.

Uncle John fists my thin T-shirt and tries to jerk me up.

Fuck this.

I toss him a few meters behind me, my Body strength doing all the work. I hear his crash landing and smirk.

I concentrate on mending the wound on my face, remembering I'm a three-point Organic here—or healer. Whatever name they use in bot world.

My lip stops throbbing. Blood discontinues flowing. I sit up, and Tiff's mottled greenish-brown eyes hold mine.

"You did this," she says, crying and laughing at the same time.

I lift a shoulder. "Didn't mean to, just *blinked*."

Aunt Tiff throws herself at me, and I catch her in my arms. Her rapid heartbeat flutters against me like a hummingbird's wings.

"I think I'm in love with you."

I pat her awkwardly. *Gawd.*

"What in the blue fuck is going on?" Gramps says in a rough voice.

Tiff leans away, swiping at her tears.

"Tell me why my best friend attacked my son and everyone is so interested in girls having periods?" Dad's eyebrows rise, his steady brown eyes pegging the group.

Sophie raises a hand with an old-fashioned tampon. "I have supplies."

How is that?

She whips out a sparkly violet purse with small hearts running rampant. It's attached to a belt loop on her denims. At her feet is a large suitcase-type orange purse.

Seriously?

Mom studies the group with a frown. "Who is having a menstrual cycle?"

Dee crosses her arms, glaring at me.

Sorry, Dee.

Screw you, bro.

I wince.

Sophie, Mom, and Tiff raise their hands.

No awkwardness. None. At. All.

Uncle John walks over stiffly, giving me a glare.

Whatever.

He sinks to his haunches beside Tiff and strokes a gentle finger along her face. "Does this mean?"

She nods, more tears falling over the dried tracks of the last.

I stand, brushing all the forest debris off my denims.

I go flying in the next moment and land on my ass again. My teeth click together, and I bite my tongue half-off.

"No, Mitchell."

I crack an eyelid open, and Deegan's zombie is bearing down on me.

We're just gonna have to go, I guess.

I leap up just as his big zombie ass barrels into me. *Fuck, but he's strong.*

We crash into a nearby tree trunk, and it snaps, throwing us into the pile of limbs and leaves as it falls behind us.

Something invisible tears us apart.

It's hilarious, too. Mitch is swinging at the air, trying to get to me.

"There's some things about this world to commend," John comments in a dry voice.

I follow the direction of his gaze, and Sophie's arms are flat out like she's ready for super hero cape land, face in hard lines of concentration as her aqua eyes slit on us. "If you bozos are done with the male testosterone fest, I'll let you down."

I can't help it; I laugh. Sophie is telekinetic here. *Unbelievable.*

Sophie drops me on my ass—from about twelve feet. "Argh!" I scream like an abused pirate, my hands cradling my ass. "You broke my butt bones, ya witch!"

Dee is suddenly there.

I scowl up at her. "I'm sorry," I grit between my teeth.

Dee grins. "You look pretty silly holding your butt cheeks, bro."

Probably. "I am, Dee. Wasn't trying to hurt your feelings."

She nods, then her face bleeds to red again. "It's just. I've never had a period before. And—gah."

Oh.

Yeah, she answers mentally.

I grab an amputated tree limb and jerk myself upright, grimacing when the torn ends stab me.

My ass is killing me.

I concentrate on healing my butt, which, yeah, was fractured in the drop. I squint at Sophie.

She smirks. "Took care of your dumb ass."

Mom scowls at her. "You didn't have to be so rough."

Sophie snorts. "You were always too soft on the kids, Jade."

Dad puts an arm around Mom's shoulders. "Son."

I nod. "I gotcha. But I know what's what. If we can avoid Thompson long enough…" I leave the rest unsaid.

So much doesn't need to be spoken aloud.

Everybody on my planet knows that the Terrans can't have kids.

Jonesy fist-pumps in the background, jerking his eyebrows up and down.

Uncle Clyde pipes in. "This is a most unseemly conversation. In my day—"

"Amen," Gramps says without encouragement, a permanent scowl affixed to his face.

Right. I throw up my hand. "Well, guys, pulseflash— those days are over. We have hardly any fertility. I *blink* us to bot world, and all the females of the group have a period."

I look at Sophie. "Normal for you?"

She blushes. *I'm just stepping in all kinds of shit.* "I've been carrying that same tampon for twenty years," she confesses in a soft voice.

"What?" Tiff asks, surprise written all over her.

Sophie lifts her chin defiantly. "I hoped. I had no man, girlfriend. Just me. And how old are we now?" She throws her palms up then slaps her thighs to punctuate her point.

Old, I think, but I'm not stupid enough to say.

Deegan carves a scathing look at me, and I just jerk my shoulders up.

I won't say anything.

Mitch strides over, and Dee puts a hand on his arm.

I watch his face soften on her.

Better not put your joystick in my sister. I shudder. Disgusting thought.

"So what we've got here are a bunch of females from our world who can't have kids. But here—they can?" Gramps asks, getting to the crux of the thing.

"Looks like," I say, spitting out the remaining blood from Uncle John's love tap and the subsequent zombie toss.

"Sorry, Pax," John says, spreading his palms away from his lean body, face flaming tomato red.

"It's okay," I mumble.

Tiff claps her hands. "This is fantastic, John," her eyes sparkle like green lamps of happiness.

"I know, spitfire." Uncle John draws her in close against him, stroking her hair.

It's Dee that doles out the bad news. Genius IQ. Sometimes, it sucks ass to be brilliant. That level of self-awareness would blow. Glad I'm just bright.

"I think we would have to… uh…" She bites her lower lip. "Engage in intercourse on this world, for it to be effective."

Dad blanches.

I scowl. At Mitch.

Dee's zombie raises a hand. "Dead guys. I'm dead. Stop looking at me like you need to kill me again."

"I do not think your status of alive or dead is relevant, young man." Uncle Clyde turns the flaps of his suit jacket away as he places his hands on his hips, regarding Mitch.

No way. "Don't you touch Dee," I say.

"Pax!" she yells at me. "Don't assume stuff."

I look at Mitch's face and see what's there. What I knew would be there. "I'll assume as much as I want."

"She's not of age, man," Mitch argues reasonably, then looks at Gramps and Dad. Finally, he narrows his sights on me. "Deegan just turned seventeen." He flicks a glance to Dee, and she opens her mouth. "No, Deegan," Mitch says in a low voice. "You're still underage."

Mom blushes. "I don't want Deegan with a zombie." She shivers.

Dad begins to move toward Mitch.

"But, she's *not* underage." Mom's voice rings with conviction, and Dad turns.

"I *will* kill any guy who touches Deegan."

That's so realistic, Dad. I roll my eyes.

Mitch crosses his arms, glaring at all the men.

A harsh laugh rockets out of Gramps. "Great sentiment, kid. But the reality is: Deegan can have sex with whoever she wants."

Dee and I groan.

Gramps. There is a thing as *too* much honesty.

"I'm not having sex with anyone! I'm having my period!"

"Thanks for the information, Deegan," a voice says from a safe distance.

I know that voice.

I turn slowly, and my breath oozes out of me.

The Brad Thompson of our world smiles. But his eyes aren't on me, Mitch, Dad, Gramps, Jonesy, Uncle John, or even Clyde.

No.

His eyes are all for the females of the group. The two I care about most in this world are included in his rapt attention.

"Don't," Thompson's eyes move toward my dad.

Dad's probably gearing up for another torch session.

My eyes move behind Thompson. A hundred zombies perch like vultures before carrion.

He hikes a weapon I don't recognize. Looks like a gun, but not. It has a big ass hole at the end, though. "I'm king of the heap here, Hart."

This guy tortured my sister. Not this Thompson, but a version of him from this world. *Hate* is not a strong enough word for what I'm feeling right now.

Mitch and I exchange a look.

Funny how all our rivalry and dickness is shelved when Dee hangs in the balance.

"Got a nice little ring of AftDs taking care of business here. I get all the flesh I want." Thompson swings his hips in a parody of a hump grind, and I close my eyes to block out the visual.

Even though my telepathy doesn't extend past my sister, I know what he wants to do to Dee, the sick fuck.

"Sorry about your penis, Thompson," Jonesy says in a bland voice.

Dee makes a distressed sound behind me.

I take her hand, the one Mitch isn't holding.

Brad tilts his head, staring at Jonesy like a bird before a worm. "Ah—Mark Jones. The stupid one of the group."

"Smart enough to know when a dude's compensating for lack of equipment." Jonesy smirks.

The back of my eyelids burn. Jonesy's not dumb.

He's brave.

"I'll make you hump half-rotten girls, Jones." Brad Thompson smiles cruelly.

Jonesy grabs his package. "That all you got, pencil prick?"

As it turns out, he's got so much more.

10

Gramps

I swipe my tongue over my shredded bottom lip.

I could use a bit of what Pax has. That Organic mumbo-jumbo would be handier than hell about now.

I lift a cuffed wrist and flex my fingers. Well, the four that aren't broken.

Seems like the old bod has just about had it.

Felt good to beat anything that got near the family, though. And there are cigarettes here.

Fabulous.

I lift the lit cig to my lips, wince at the murderous agony of my wounded mouth, and suck a drag. I tilt my head, tense at the permanent kink in my neck, and shoo the smoke out in a steady stream.

"Thought you guys were advanced in 2049?" Mitch asks absently, studying my nasty little habit.

He looks about how I feel. But zombies can't feel pain. I snort. *Liked Mitch's work on Thompson's horde.*

That was a class-A beatdown. *Yesiree.*

But half his head is missing, and Mitch reeks. Bad. He's an aggressive sucker. They came for Deedie, and without a sound, Mitch dropped that little girl's hand and charged into the horde.

Brad Thompson watched with a vague smile on his miserable face.

Then Caleb set him on fire. *That* was choice.

I take another drag, letting my fractured wrist dangle on my bent knee, where it throbs in time with my heart-beat. My old ass joins in with the all-over hurt against the cement cell floor, where we all sit in a row, each separated by bars.

Then Thompson's Null showed up, and while the zombies restrained my grandson (with his absolute lack of AftD on bot world), they took Jade, Tiff, Sophie, and Deedie.

We tried to reason with Thompson.

I chuckle. *Not really,* we just tried to kill his ass. The Nulls all seem to be the same on every world, stealing everyone's paranormal juice. And with his fleet of pow-erful Nulls—and Caleb's lack of the death juice—we weren't worth squat.

Mitch raises an eyebrow. I study him for a moment; he looks like a former military man. I think I caught sight of some dog tags flying around in the fracus.

I answer his earlier question. "Advanced? Yeah. I like my smokes. It's about options, Mitch."

Caleb rolls his head where he lies on the floor, one eyeball finding me. "Thompson likes you smoking."

"He's a sissy-sucking titty baby," I comment in a bald voice.

Caleb chokes a laugh, but blood comes out instead of sound. They worked my grandson over pretty good. He's got one good eye; the other is swollen shut. Probably internal injuries.

Definitely.

We could all use a dose of Organic right now. I frown. The Jezebel of this world became a zombie that Caleb had to burn to death later. Damn unfortunate.

I sigh. *Guess she's off the list.* "But," I say, flicking a long ash to the left of where we all sit in rows, "this jagup holds the reins on our freedom."

Mitch hisses, and Clyde nods in succinct agreement. Zombie unity. It's a beautiful thing.

I crush out the cig and shake my hands. The pain flares. I breathe through it. Miserable.

Jonesy is unconscious. Don't know how much hope we have of him ever waking up.

When Brad grabbed Sophie's breast, Jones went berserk. Well, more berserk than usual.

He got a couple of nice licks in before four of the horde took him down.

"Gramps," Caleb calls quietly.

Full of shit I can't address—or fix.

"Master," Clyde says, half in mourning, half in comfort.

Caleb's one good eye shuts at the tone in his voice.

They've got our ladies. And there's nothing that feels good about that.

Especially Dee. Thompson's got a Null stationed on her so she can't call anything to help her and the other girls.

Speaking of Nulls. I glance at Terran, who's out cold too. He and Jones took exception to them hauling Tiff and Sophie off.

Great exception. *Imagine that?*

We have our very own Null, as well.

He sits on a stool, perched in the corner of our partially submerged subterranean prison.

His cowboy hat is slung low, covering most of his eyes. The little that I can see stares at us with complete disinterest.

I take mental stock of who we have. All the guys are in various states of compromise. None of us escaped beatings.

Seems like tradition for the Harts, as well as the guys who hang out with a Hart.

Pax is doing the best as he healed the majority of his damage with his three-point Organic ability.

Good thing. He just about died. Body or no Body, he sustained a lot of damage. Too many damn zombies.

Determined fuckers.

And did I mention Brad Thompson's a three-point AftD here? The hits just keep on coming.

This nutjob is related to that chump who assaulted Tiff back in the day. What was his name? *Ah, Carson Hamilton.*

There we were, assuming that Thompson's little vendetta was because of Deedie's rejection (like that would be enough to allow his cheese to slide of his cracker). After all, everyone in her age bracket was scarce. Males still want females. And if there aren't many to be had?

Well some putzes just don't understand *no.*

Thompson's dad had been a cousin to Hamilton's father. *Ain't it just all cozy?*

For an almost nineteen-year-old kid, he's as sideways as they come. A real loon. Entitled punk gets a little power, and suddenly, he stumbles across a girl that said no, and gets the idea of holding the entire family hostage.

There's no recourse in bot world. At least young Brad had to *pretend* to mind himself on our earth.

The Hart family here are zombies, already killed by the Thompsons of this world.

Seems like the parallel dimensions repeat the same scenes in different ways.

I wonder absently what the other Macs are like, and the thought makes me an internal shudder. One of me is plenty.

Then this hot little number walks in, and I enjoy the view, since I can't save the girls.

Yet.

I'm actually nearing eight-five years old in real age. But because of the regeneration that seemed to take hold so strongly, I look mid-fifties. Doesn't work with all folks. Kinda like transplants that don't take when the body rejects them. My body likes transplants (already had two lung replacements), and the bod definitely took like a duck to water with the regeneration.

So I don't feel too bad distracting myself from our miserable circumstances when a late-forties hottie walks into our cell group.

Mitch and Clyde give her a passing glance. Pax snorts, looking down at his sneakers.

Kid's as pissed as a monkey that can't throw shit.

I check her out as she moves past the cells. Got weight in all the right places. Good thing, too, because I've never been on board with that rail-thin look. I like a woman with curves. "Tits and ass," we used to say in the day and would get flogged for admitting now. Same holds true, I imagine, even in our "enlightened" times.

I chuckle, and the woman glances my way with a tentative smile.

She's got the chow, so she's not unpopular.

The Null sits up straighter. "Put the food here, Kim. Don't need you getting next to these criminals."

I grunt. That's rich. Yeah—*we're* the criminals. I glare at his lying ass, and he tips his cowboy hat at me. I'd love to heal up and give him a go.

Cowboy Null sees something on my face that causes him to frown.

Yeah, think on that, numb nuts.

My gaze moves back to Kim of the sweet hourglass figure, and she kicks up her chin. "They need you upstairs, Ron."

Oooh—dismissal, *chump*.

He shakes his head. "Nah, Brad won't like me straying too far."

She puts a hand on her hip, and I take note of how well her jeans fit. Really well.

"Not Null enough?" she asks in a coy voice.

He jerks to a stand, and every man who's conscious tenses. We know potential for male violence—second nature to those men who are tapped into their primal potential.

"Shut up, Kim." He glares, looming over her shorter frame.

She stands her ground.

Damn, I like 'em feisty.

I'm as tense as a cat in a room full of rockers, waiting to see if this simp will hurt a woman. Seems like anything's possible on this rock.

"I'm here to deliver food. Word from above is they need two Nulls to subdue the teenage girl."

I perk up at that. *Deedie. They're talking about our Deedie.*

I'm not the only one that notices. Mitch's eyes are lead weights on Null boy. Quick as a snake, Cowboy Null grabs her wrist.

"Hey!" I croak from my parched throat.

The Null looks at me. I feel the weight of his power, but I'm a mundane, so his stuff is wasted on me.

"Mind your own business."

"Make me," I say like a juvenile. Feels right as rain.

His eyes slim down on me, and he makes to move around Kim as she tries to yank her hand away. "Stop throwing your weight around, Ron. I'm the messenger."

He ignores me and focuses on Kim again. *Damn.* "Yeah, I got that. If you weren't a relative, I'd teach you a lesson about respect."

She jerks her wrist in a circle, and Ron drops it. "But I am. And for the record, respect is earned."

He chuckles. "Or forced."

"Just go," Kim says in a low voice.

Ron stares at her a moment longer, then with a scathing glance at the males who are awake, he saunters out.

"Clown," Pax mutters as the door clanks behind him.

Good food smells waft through the cell, and my mouth waters. Funny how a man's appetite waits for no one. I find the consistency humorous.

Kim meets my eyes. And she's a plain woman, one of those gals who are all ripe and lush body—except for her eyes. The lack of interesting features of her face melt away around her eyes.

They're not a special color. Just brown.

But they're beautiful, soulful. I can see how she feels down to her toenails and that kind of vulnerability is bad. Bad for her.

Maybe good for us.

Her interaction with Ron the Null has shown there's dissent in the ranks, and that's a wedge I hope to widen.

She blows out a harsh breath, and the movement lifts her chestnut hair, which has a few strands of tinsel in the ranks.

I wonder at her exact age. For the first time in years, I wonder how a woman would feel underneath me again.

Boners are part of the regeneration process.

Happy day.

Of course, hard-ons aren't really the priority at the moment. But I've never met a dick that cooperates. Never have, never will. Pricks get hard at the most inopportune times imaginable.

Like now.

I use my left hand to apply pressure to the busted finger on my right. The pain chases away the untimely and uninvited lust.

What the hell is wrong with me? Oh yeah, last year, I had all the impulses of an old guy. Now the Viagra of back in the day isn't necessary.

I smile. *Feels good to be back.* Even in the middle of this colossal clusterfuck.

A ghost of a smile crosses my lips. Nothing makes a gent feel more alive than food on a plate and an upright Johnson in the trousers.

Now, to get out of this current disaster and get to rescuing the girls.

Those brown eyes survey the less-than-friendly crowd. "I guess you know by now, I'm Kim."

We just look at her. Ball's in her court.

She doesn't wring her hands, but her eyes are the tell to how nervous she is.

"I'm-I'm Brad's first cousin once removed, and in charge of food delivery to the…" She stumbles a little on this because the young prince has been pretty transparent. He's a puppet of his old man, a genuine criminal—world notwithstanding. "Inmates," she finishes, her large brown eyes wide in her face.

Seeing me, she comes to my cell first. I must look to be the most harmless of the group.

Wrong.

Kim hunches over with the tray. I get a load of her great cleavage from the tight T-shirt with a row of little buttons on the top that bisect a well-developed rack.

I beat down my wood again with a mental thought of the women who need saving, and I go to neutral again. Figures this bullshit has to happen right now.

"I'll push the food through, and you take it."

Seems simple.

Except that I've worked the cuff of my right hand loose. Broken fingers aid that whole escape angle.

The zombies know.

Not sure how. But they do. Clyde's and Mitch's bright eyes never leave me.

Brains in sight. I bite back my chuckle.

Kim slides the food tray through a slot positioned just above the cement floor, and I shoot forward. My reflexes were always cat-like when I was a young man. In the corp, my nickname was Tom. For Tomcat.

That speed has come back, along with the waning vestiges of my youth.

I latch on to the wrist that Ron the Null just had, and Kim yelps. Fear lurches into those lovely velvety-chocolate eyes, and guilt sweeps me.

I do not want to hurt a woman to save ours. Had that protective instinct since I was born. Can't shake it. But I might be able to fake it.

Then a wondrous thing happens. My wounds melt, my heartbeats stutter over one another, and my broken finger straightens around her dainty wrist.

Our eyes meet. "Well, well—what do we have here?"

Big alligator tears crawl down her face. "Don't tell him," she whispers.

My forehead screws into a frown, but my grip remains tight. "Tell who?"

"Brad," she whispers.

I lean forward to catch her words and notice amber flecks within the deep-brown sea of her irises. "That I'm a Healer."

I ask an instinctive question, "Did you want to heal me?"

The corners of her lips turn up. "Why do you think I sent that smug asshole Ron packing?"

We grin at each other, and her tears dry.

I don't mean to stroke the skin of her wrist when I release it, but sometimes, a man's just not in charge of his actions.

Like when a beautiful woman brings food and heals him in one fell swoop.

Kim heals us.

She feeds us.

And I fall a little in love that day.

Didn't know it then. But when it came time to save the girls, it was never a question that Kim would be one of them.

Deegan

Brad tosses the menstrual cleansers inside our cells. "Have at it, ladies."

I glare.

I'll just sit here and bleed. I'm not taking off my denims to apply the cleanser in front of this loser.

His lips twist. "Get hot." Brad Thompson's large eyes move across me, Mom, Sophie, and Tiff. He's so handsome, it's painful. Someone that beautiful *should* be that way on the inside.

But he's not. He oozes narcissism. The only world Brad lives in is the world of *him*.

"Go fuck yourself, delinquent."

Guess who says that? I look at Aunt Tiff, and Brad's doe eyes, so feminine in an utterly masculine face, narrow on her. "I don't give a shit that you're a chick, just so ya know. I'll treat you just like the dudes."

"And *I* don't give any fucks that you can't find your pathetic pecker." Tiff flutters her eyelashes.

Brad jerks his chin back. Smiles. "Looked into you, Tiffany Weller."

I'm concerned about how quickly Brad switches gears. I make a studious effort not to look at Mom.

Tiff's sullen silence reigns. She's not going to give him a centimeter.

Brad steps closer to the bars. "Heard my cousin got a slice of the Tiff pie before your mess of a husband got him. Illegally."

Tiff pales. "There's nothing messy about John," she says in a low voice.

Brad lifts a muscular shoulder, dismissing her. "Don't know; he's not conscious right now."

If his words bother Aunt Tiff, I can't tell. She's gotta be the hardest woman I've ever met.

Brad's long fingers wrap the metal bars that separate us from him. "I know you can't have kids." He snorts. "What are you? Forty-one? Forty-two? Kind of long in the tooth to still want what only youth can provide. But now you've got a chance." Brad places his fingers close together, a millimeter apart.

He whirls suddenly and walks toward the opposite wall, where deeply inset, narrow windows ride close to the low ceiling.

Legs pound by outside the windows as unknowing and continuous foot traffic flows. Mostly bot, some human.

Tears burn my eyeballs. A lump forms in my throat.

I want to call the dead to me so bad, I taste their rot on my tongue.

My eyes move from Brad's back to the corner where the Null stares back. The corners of his lips tweak. "Don't even try it, Undead Princess."

Dick. I fold my arms, glaring at him.

Brad grips the bottom of the windowsill, talking to the legs that stream endlessly past. "It doesn't have to be John Terran."

Tiff's arms drop. "What, freak?"

I close my eyes. Aunt Tiff truly says whatever she wants. But in this case, it might be ill-advised.

The Null's lips curl tighter, and my heart rate picks up. He's seen the Brad Show before—and maybe liked it.

"If you're truly fertile again—and man, do I hope you are—your husband doesn't have to do the deed. The process can be any viable male. Dead or alive."

Tiff stands, rushing the bars. She grabs them, rattling them in their housing.

Mom and I exchange an uneasy glance.

Brad smiles. "Must have a touch of Body in this world." He pushes off the wall, his face going blank for a moment.

The zombies file in through the door.

Sophie moans in the background, lifting her tear-stained face from her folded arms. "I can't do this," she whispers.

Brad taps the end of Tiff's nose, and the sound of her teeth clicking are loud in the quiet as she snaps at his finger.

"I don't think you'll be the doer, Sophie," he comments absently, giving Tiff a guarded look.

Mom's hand slides through the bars, and I take it.

She knows how I feel, and Mom's a powerful Empath in this world. Her ability's been restored to a five-point.

Though Mom had me and Pax a million years ago, this world messes with all of us, causing fertility on women who are facing menopause just around the corner.

Mom and I watch the zombies—they look so alive.

"Meet my pimps, ladies."

My eyes travel the male zombies, all of them as big as Pax and Mitchell.

"Brad," I plead in a quiet voice, "Don't do this."

His small smile brightens his face again. "I need you, Deegan Hart. I need your power. For some reason, I don't have AftD anywhere but here."

I don't say that with Pax, there'd be an infinite amount of Brad's because he could *blink* him anywhere. The thought ripens gooseflesh like hills of misery on my skin. If he doesn't have Pax, he can't travel anywhere else. And in our world, though we use a zombie slave force for menial jobs and tasks, we're not creating brothels. I didn't realize until just then that there are degrees of morality.

I swallow hard, my throat clicking. "I can't give you my ability, Brad."

"But our child could."

Mom's fingers tighten on mine.

Oh my God. Is he kidding?

I look at that GQ model face. "I don't—I won't *ever* be with you, Brad."

He nods happily. "I know. That's why my zombies are here. They can give the right encouragement."

This horde doesn't shamble; they stride smoothly to the bars.

Mom and I stand, our hands laced together. The metal heats against our twined fingers.

The zombies look on solemnly, hearing only Brad's voice. His will.

I open up the well of my death power. It beats against them, and they twitch like one body.

"Narco," Brad clips.

"Got it."

Cool swamps the heat of my power. The Null in the corner, named for the drug lords of the twentieth, grins.

The zombies harden before me.

Tiff backs away.

They tear the bars from their moorings and step inside.

"Cut the melodrama, Brad," Tiff bites, but her eyes are tight with fear.

Blood runs down my leg. I guess my first menstrual period is the least of my concerns.

One zombie raises his nose to scent the air, and I shiver.

"Blood," it says. His head tips down, and his soulless eyes find mine, roving to gaze at my head.

I know what it's thinking.

So does Brad. He wags his finger at the enthusiastic zombie. "Now, now, you can't kill her, yet."

The zombie trembles with want, tantalized by my lovely brains filling my skull.

"I think I believe in reincarnation," Aunt Tiff says.

I guess for her, she's reliving the nightmare of Carson Hamilton.

But this isn't some pyrokinetic from before. This guy has unlimited resources in bot world. He wants more power. He wants what he can't have.

Me.

"Take them."

Brad glances at the menstrual cleansers, and his nose scrunches.

My eyes roam his body. He resembles one of the convicts I raised on my earth.

I think of the Reflectives from Papilio. They can't Reflect or jump—whatever they call it here because this is a parallel of our world. What did they call it? Oh yeah, Sector Three. But this world could use a little justice. They have zombie prostitutes here.

I study the zombies with barely contained horror.

Bot world has zombie pimps. When we narrowly escaped this world, I shied from thinking about. I didn't really have the time for contemplation. It was onward and upward, toward the next disaster. Bringing unsanctioned zombies from this world to ours had thrown us to the sanction wolves in my home world. I'm certain they're still searching for us.

The elder Thompson has left his prodigal son in charge of this area of power.

No one but Organics are allowed. Their version is Healers.

My head snaps to attention as Tiff roundhouse kicks the closest zombie.

I back up against the wall, my hand and Mom's straining between the bars.

The zombie's head cants to the left, and I cover my mouth with my free hand.

The other zombie moves in, grabbing Tiff, and wraps his arms around her, containing her limbs.

She kicks the next one in the chest, and he flies three meters. His body hits the wall so hard that dust from the stone foundation falls like ashy tears.

Brad's laughter is the only sound besides Tiff's pants whispering together as she scissors her legs to escape three zombies.

And she's clearly a Body in this world. But even a Body can't overpower three zombies.

I could've warned her. But Aunt Tiff already knew. She just won't listen. She can't. Tiff's not hardwired to give up.

They take her down. Blood stains her jeans as she squirms. "You fuckers!" Tiff screams, biting the arm that holds her. She spits the chunk of undead flesh, and it lands with a wet smack on the concrete floor.

The one constant: *Zombies don't feel pain.*

I feel her AftD well, and mine mingles with hers.

Narco flexes his Null muscle, and I drop to my knees.

Mitchell! I scream, still clutching Mom's hand.

He doesn't hear me.

Pax!

A handful of seconds pound by. Then: *Dee!*

My eyes fly open. My head whips to Mom. *Help,* I mouth.

She nods.

I think.

Mom sends images through our amplified connection to Pax.

My brother's rage is tasteable.

"What the *fuck* are you doing, Deegan?" Brad seethes, his pretty-boy face turning ugly in a heartbeat.

I don't break my concentration for a second. I keep *sending.*

His slap on my cheek rocks my head against the wall, and my visual stream trembles. I *send.*

"Don't you hit my baby," Mom says.

Brad's face whips to Narco. "Are you even fucking trying?"

Narco's small eyes become slits of hate. "You try holding back this much AftD and see how it works. I can't keep *all* their abilities locked down."

Brad grunts, and my palm hits the solid rock wall behind me before I slide down.

"Fine, get the Cowboy."

Narco's lips lift. "Already sent Cousin Kim."

Brad's lips lift off his brilliant white teeth. "Tight."

Narco's shoulders relax.

Spittle flies from Tiff's lips, "Release me!"

I throw my death energy in with hers.

No, Pax says.

Have to try, I reply.

Suddenly, I can feel Mitchell. He and Pax are touching.

Hi, Mitchell. I feel the goofy smile form on my face, while the taste of copper sears my cut lip.

Deegan.

I breathe him in. Whatever combination makes Mitchell mine threads through me. His strength. His essence.

I don't really even feel Brad hit me again. The room tilts, and I fall on my side. Brad's shoes are all I see.

Mom's screams hurt my ears.

"You cowardly sonofabitch!" Tiff screams.

Scuffles reach me, then mumbled bits of cursing.

Then silence.

Large feet join Brad's.

Mom's hand is torn from mine, and there are no pictures now. Only words.

Help.

Brad grabs my wrist. He drags me across the floor, and the blood from my cycle leaves a trail behind me.

I'm still me enough to be mortified.

Sophie screams, and Mom joins her. The harmony of their fear paralyzes my own.

Dad and Pax would kill these guys. That's why they separated us, I guess.

Brad gets me out the cell door, and the zombie's follow. Their feet follow anyway.

As I'm dragged past Tiff, I scramble for her hand.

Brad hits her with his fist.

Tiff goes down, her knee hitting the cement floor, hard. She smiles up at him for a split-second, her teeth lined by red, and strikes out with her hand, nailing Brad in the crotch. His knees buckle.

Tiff bounds up.

"Subdue her," Brad says in a low voice full of intent.

Tiff kicks him in the teeth. "No more pretty boy." She breathes the words through her pain.

Brad lands backward, hands clutching his balls as blood flies in an arc toward the low ceiling.

I crawl toward the Null.

Narco backs away. "No touchy," he murmurs.

I put everything I am into the one command. I don't know all that I am here, but I'll be damned if I let Brad force me to watch him take apart the people I love.

I lurch forward from my hands and knees, my hands encircling his ankle.

Narco tries to kick me and lands a solid hit on my shoulder. Agony sings through the joint, causing me to grit my teeth.

A zombie hand grabs my ankle, and I feel my abilities in my mind like a deck of playing cards.

I shuffle, dismiss my surprised irony at what I hope will help us the most, and give the command, "Narco, silence Brad Thompson."

Narco stills.

The zombie jerks me backward, and I fight to latch on to any part of the Null.

A yawning mouth full of square yellow teeth draws nearer, aiming for my neck.

"Subdue!" Brad shrieks the garbled command from his position on the floor.

I hear a tearing sound and jerk away from the zombies' mouth in time to watch Narco duct-tape Brad's mouth.

Narco stands from his bent position over Brad.

Holy shit. "Don't bite me," I command the zombie, whose hot rotting breath bathes the lower half of my jaw.

His forward movement arrests like a pulse switched to *off.* The dead's eyes roll to meet mine. "Mistress."

I've never heard a word I liked better in my entire life.

"Release me."

He does, and I barely catch my body from smacking the concrete. Zombies are so literal. The undead guy never thought about letting me down gently—or slowly. The command was given; the zombie complied.

I turn to Brad, who's writhing on the floor, rocking back and forth while holding his crotch. His eyes bulge with the need to talk.

Oh, what he would say—no, command—if he were able. But he's not.

I want to feel superior, but all I can manage is profound relief.

Mom runs to me, her eyes rolling over my body, clearly checking for injuries. There're plenty. I can feel my face already swelling from the slaps. "Did you get control of the zombies, Deegan?"

I laugh—*control*—and the sound becomes a sob.

I nod quickly, tears scattering like errant rain. I stand and sway. Mom slides her arm around my waist. We're the same size, so I lean against her, grateful for the support.

Sophie walks up to me, and I note we're all filthy, bleeding like stuck pigs while Narco keeps adding layers of tape over Brad's mouth.

Wow, love that. I give a weary smile. *Took my command to heart.* I suck in a gasping inhale. "That's enough, Narco."

He gives an absent smile and stands. He sways slightly, awaiting further instruction.

I shiver in distaste.

"How did you know?" Mom asks, searching my face.

That I was a Manipulator in this world? "I didn't." I try to regulate my breathing so I don't hyperventilate.

"So for goddamned once, we get lucky?" Tiff struggles to stand, beaten up but whole. "About damn time." The corners of her mouth rise, and she kicks Brad in the ribs.

I jump at the violence.

His muffled yell is audible through the tape. His beautiful large dove gray eyes are wide.

Aunt Tiff gives a decisive nod. "I feel better now."

Mom frowns. Her hands shake as she tucks my mostly loose hair out of my face. Her hands clasp the sides of my cheeks. "Deegan."

The zombies shudder. My face whips to them. They have an alert edge that I didn't put there. "Someone's coming."

Brad goes silent.

Narco is still vacant. "Who else knows about us?" I ask while giving him a nice mental shove.

His left eye twitches. "Only the other AftDs and Brad's dad."

Other AftDs.

We need to go. I wrap my fingers around Mom's arm to speed our communication, and her eyes get round. "Okay," she breathes, getting my sense of urgency through the Empath Highway.

Sophie makes a sound of fear low in her throat. "I want Jonesy."

I swipe a tear from my face. *I want them all.*

"Let's get the fuck outta Dodge, girls," Tiff says. She heads for the door and tears it open. One of the hinges comes away from the jamb. "Damn, I love this Body thing. Gonna suck to have to go back to my weak-ass body in our earth."

If we get back.

As we leave, I send out the feelers.

Pax pings back immediately.

I move in that direction, one hand clutching the menstrual cleansers.

A girl has to be practical.

12

Pax

Gramps has got his eye on Kim, who's a closet Organic—or "Healer," as they're called on bot world. She's not a Brad fan, too, as it turns out, and she wastes no time after Cowboy Null leaves, to heal us out of the worst of our injuries.

"He's worse than our Brad was." Kim's fingers tighten on Gramps's last wound, where deep abrasions cross his hands.

"How is he getting away with this zombie brothel thing?" Gramps asks.

Kim's large brown eyes take in the foot traffic cruising past the window. "I don't know exactly how it all began—I was young. There was a scientist team responsible for inventing the first cyber technology."

Gramps snorts, giving us guys a full look. "Remember their names?"

Kim bites her thumbnail. Her once-tidy hair has come undone into a curling mass of dark-brown hair with a few gray strands. She pushes a tendril behind her ear and replies, "Zoe-something." Her eyes roll toward the ceiling, clearly trying to remember. "Zon—darack?" Kim gives a small shake of her head. "That's not quite right."

"Zondorae," Dad supplies in a cryptic tone.

Great.

She flashes a brilliant smile at him and snaps her fingers. Fingers that made us all well. "That's it, thanks."

All of us guys exchange another loaded glance. Except Mitch. He doesn't have the history to understand the implications.

So the Zondoraes are mad scientists in *this* world, too. Figures. Instead of just messing with all the teens here, they also had their fingers in the cyber pie.

Fucking swell.

Kim waves away her words. "So they began making cyborgs—prototypes. 'Small nonessentials,' I believe they were called. And eventually, the cyborgs became larger, more complex. After time, they evolved enough to take over the manual labor force. So the sanctioning of zombies for a workforce never materialized." Her face grows sad. "But that didn't stop Clement Thompson from harnessing the sex trade potential of the undead."

Brad's dad.

"I'm not embarrassed," Kim says. "Not at all." Her face flames.

Mitch glowers, and Jonesy, still sitting on his ass in the corner of the cell—now awake—rubs his chest. "Sounds like necrophilia any way you slice it." He ignores the emotional vibe and goes straight for the bottom-line jugular.

Dad's lips quirk.

Jonesy gives Dad an incinerating stare. "Fuck off, Hart. When it comes to anything sex-related, I know my business." He thumbs his chest. "Except for Alex. Now *that* dude is knowledgeable."

Disgusting.

"Okay, I'd really like to know more," Gramps says, ignoring their exchange, "but we need to find the girls."

Kim's face pinches, and a large tear seeps out of her eye. "I might be a Thompson, but just because I'm Clem's first cousin doesn't mean I'll be given any latitude for letting you go." She bites her thumbnail again. "Healing you is a compulsive ability. I feel ill if I don't use it. But they might kill me—or worse—if I let you guys go. Relative or not. *And,* I've kept my ability a secret."

She doesn't say why, but I don't have to be a brain surgeon to figure it out. Thompson would exploit his own mother if it advanced his goals. Dicklick.

We're silent. Obviously, all our wheels are turning. Don't want to get anyone's ass in a sling because we're trying to escape. But I'm not looking forward to joining some kind of zombie ranks or whatever else that fuck-knuckle Brad can cook up.

Gramps tilts his head to the side, capturing his chin with a hand bearing only faded bruises now. "Why don't you come with us? You could use your ability out in the open in our world, and you wouldn't have to be the lackey for your sick family."

Go, Gramps.

Kim's lower lip trembles. "*If* I left"—she shakes her head, hair scattering from its binding and falling around her shoulders—"and they ever find me…" Her body shakes.

Gramps's expression softens. "They don't have a *blinker* here, do they?"

Kim shakes her head.

"Or a Dimensional?" His salt-and-pepper eyebrows rise slowly.

"God no!" she laughs as if that's a ridiculous question.

I don't really think the question is that out there. I expect vampires and shit to ooze out of the cement at any time. They *do* have bots here, and zombie whorehouses. Is the possibility of a Dimensional a big stretch?

"So we go—you come with—and bye-bye bot world." Gramps gives a mock-wave.

"Why do you keep calling it 'bot world'?" Kim's forehead wrinkles between her eyes.

Gramps shrugs. "I don't know, but saying *cyborg* every time one of those bag of bolts opens its mouth to shriek takes time. Don't feel like giving it. Color me lazy."

Kim laughs. She and Gramps gaze at each other for a few seconds. "Okay," she says softly. "I don't have a husband or kids here."

Gramps's face doesn't give anything away, but I'm pretty sure he's crushing on Kim, which is too surreal for me to inspect closely.

I shake off my bullshit. "Are there fertility problems here?" I ask, sure that there isn't since all the females of our group started cycling practically as soon as we got here. And Dee never had before.

"No." Kim shakes her head. "Fertility's no issue, but the population is on the decline." She lifts her shoulder.

"Why have children when the bots do everything that humans were needed for in the past?" John Terran comments slowly.

Kim nods. "And zombies provide sex for money." Her voice is pretty bland. Guess the deal's been going on for a while here, so people are used to it.

"Who gets the money for that horrible trade?" Dad folds his arms, planting his feet wide apart.

Kim rolls her eyes and replies quietly, "All compensation goes to Thompson Enterprises."

"So what if the zombies are aware?"

All eyes go to Mitch.

He regards us in turn. "I mean, if Dee said I had to have... *relations* with some girl, I'd *have* to—even if I didn't want to. But I'd know I was doing something against my will." He looks at each of us.

"Too true, my friend," Clyde says.

The two zombies exchange a glance of perfect understanding.

And that's when I notice Clyde is decaying. *Bobbi Gale isn't here.*

"Dad," I say, jerking my jaw at Uncle Clyde.

Dad casts his eyes at the floor. "I know, dammit."

"Still no AftD, son?" Gramps asks.

Dad shakes his head, his hands falling to fists at his sides. "Just a bunch of wildcard pyro. Feel like a toddler with a lighter."

Whatever a lighter is.

There's no one to keep Clyde "alive" anymore. Dee and Tiff aren't here. And for some reason, only Bobbi and Dad can give him the juice to remain in perfect form.

This is sucking ass.

Pax!

I jump half a meter. Dee's scream is like a pulseified cattle prod up my ass.

"What was *that*?" Dad pulls a curious face at my sudden jerk.

Moving to the bars that separate all of us, John and Jonesy stare at me.

I don't answer because I can't. Images are flowing, and I can taste that Mom is driving this particular telepath freight train.

But I don't get bogged down in the *how*. I'm sort of a reactive type.

The images my sister *sends* scare the shit out of me. Brad is there, threatening Dee with zombie gang rape. The women are being bullied.

Knowing I'm responsible for bringing us back to bot world makes my blood boil. Basically, I served Dee up to Thompson on a silver platter.

I need to get to Dee. I reach for Mitch, and he doesn't hesitate. Our hands connect, and he sees what I'm seeing. Feels what I'm feeling.

His face goes murderous. And that figures since he is a murderer. And Mitch will be one again if he needs to bring it. Deadly force.

Everyone starts talking at once.

"Is Soph okay—"

"Tiff can't be…" John groans, putting his head in his hands.

"Where's Deedie?" Gramps's concerned face floats into view.

But Mitch and I have gone deep, and we clench palms in a grip so tight it hurts even me, a Body.

Kim's frightened voice says, "What's he doing? Are they coming back?"

I grit my teeth. *Gotta get out of here.*

I watch through Dee's eyes as Tiff kicks Brad's teeth in. Then Dee twists on the floor while a zombie jerks her back from a Null. Has to be a Null; my senses tell me he's a big void in the room.

Teeth bear down on my sister. Chompers loom large as they advance toward her neck.

"No," I breathe out. He'll kill her with a single bite.

"No," Mitch echoes in a hiss, hand convulsing around mine.

"Let's fucking go and get the chicks," Jonesy says, looking at Mitch and me.

Sweat rolls down my face.

"Yeah." I lift my chin and tear my hand out of Mitchell's grasp.

Clyde, gray-skinned, with eyes that roll in his sockets, nods. "We will retrieve Deegan."

My eyes rove his compromised body. "You might stand out, Uncle Clyde."

He tilts his head to the side and hisses, mouth dark. "It will not be the first time, young Master."

Gramps looks to Kim, who's a little green around the gills, as he would say. "I know that you're scared sweetheart, but we won't hurt you. Might even give you a new lease on life."

She gnaws her lower lip, giving Clyde a well-deserved look of fear. "I won't have a life if I'm caught."

I grin, and Kim gives me a puzzled look, reluctantly taking her eyes from Clyde.

"I don't think Brad's up to much right now."

She sighs in relief. "Maybe that'll buy us time."

Or not.

Kim takes old-fashioned keys off the wall—the large brass loop holds about a dozen—and unlocks us all.

"No pulse technology?" Uncle John asks, surprised.

Kim turns to him. The keys make metallic music as she gestures with her hands. "Pulse what?"

John smiles. "They've got bots, and Zondorae's interference—"

"And the Helix Strand—their version of the Helix Complex." Dad is tossing his words over his shoulder, already moving toward the door.

"But no pulse." I can't believe what kind of bogus systems they have to be using to communicate.

Gramps doesn't waste any time from being freed, walking straight for Kim, and she backs up against the wall. "Please don't hurt me."

I know Gramps won't hurt her.

But her reaction tells me where chicks fall in the hierarchy of this world.

Gramps halts then chuckles. "I'm not gonna hurt ya. I'm gonna lay one on ya."

Seriously?

"What—" she stutters, flattening her palm against the stone wall.

Then Gramps pulls her against him and kisses her on the mouth.

Not great timing for a romance.

But I figure Gramps is gonna make the most of his golden years or something. No matter what world we're in.

"Gramps," Dad says, interrupting.

"Mhmm," he mumbles, macking with Kim, and she twines her arms around his neck.

Huh.

"Let's go." Dad has his hand on the knob to freedom.

Gramps pulls away, taking a strand of Kim's hair that got caught between them, and tucks it behind her ear.

Kim appears to be in a stupor, face flushed, eyes wide, breaths coming fast.

"Way to go, Mac," Jonesy says in a dry voice.

I turn, and he shoots a tired fist-pump into the air. "Love that you're digging the ladies and all, but it's time to get *our* girls, ya old perv."

Gramps grins. "Yup, but I'm a believer in timing."

"Ah-huh." Jonesy smirks.

Then Cowboy returns, and everything goes to hell.

Cowboy

Ron moves with his usual quiet grace to where the other-world females are being held.

In the beginning, being the pet Null of Thompson Enterprises was king of fun. Brad was a sick fuck, but everything he did was legal. The cyborgs flipped burgers and picked up human refuse. Contemporary humans enjoyed a life where all our needs were summarily accomplished without us lifting a finger.

If a guy got horny, there was a brothel at every street corner—like the narcotics and alcohol bars of the past, brothels were a stone's throw from where a human could partake in the high of their choice and nail a little undead pussy—or cock. The Zondorae scientists made traditional labor obsolete.

Money was an archaic holdover that no longer mattered. People were assigned the same amount of credits annually, and cyborgs did everything we didn't want to do.

Of course, man still wanted to fuck and eat. Bots couldn't do that.

Then Ron's Thompson Enterprises changed hands, and now we have a new Brad. This troupe of other-world paranormals blasted in and murdered the old Brad and burnt the Brad Thompson of this world to a crisp. Old Bacon Brad. I chuckle.

The Zondoraes were a busy pair, concocting a potion that allowed genetic markers for what was coined "sixth sense attributes" to manifest in a particular segment of the human population. The part of the human population struggling through the small window of puberty.

Simultaneously, the cyborg technology they'd been cultivating took an evolutionary leap forward and coincidentally came online when all the kiddies popped their abilities. The two technologies coupling turned out to be very bad timing.

Zondorae backpedaled when fifteen-year-old pimply faced boys began setting fire to everyone who pissed them off. No frontal lobe maturity and a huge amount of testosterone was a shitty mix.

And then there were the Manipulators. They were the first to get cleaned.

I can't help the grim smile that screws itself onto my face. It was a fucking *thing*. I shudder at the memories.

The solitary reason my ass stayed out of the camps for paranormals was that as a Null, I couldn't Manipulate dick, though I *could* limit the powers of all paranormals. Helix Strand made sure to find every Null higher than a level three and press them into service.

Even if they didn't *want* to give their service.

But this new Brad makes the former seem reasonable. This guy.

This guy.

He's got a pack of rats in his attic. And Clement Thompson, also an other-world transplant, is just fine with letting his almost-nineteen-year-old son be in charge of the zombie brothels in our region.

Zombies can take a fuckton of damage. If there's an AftD powerful enough, there's almost no limit to the injury-repair cycle. That type of scene is very popular to a certain group.

Except that zombies know what's happening to them.

And the new Brad is making noise about doing other things. Things I can't think about.

Then there's this dude named Parker and his twin from the other world.

I gotta make a stand. Get out of this world. The cyborgs are run by a mainframe, which is also artificial intelligence. And as soon as they don't need my level-five Nullness, I'm expendable.

There's no help here with the new Thompson regime.

13

Deegan

I scramble out of the holding cell and take a short climb of stairs two at a time. My eyes travel a long corridor devoid of people.

Old checkered vinyl tiles run like two-tone ugly diamonds of dull rust and cream down a path that gives no clue to the correct direction for escape. Weak sunlight stretches through sparkly glass windows.

Probably cleaned by bots. I shiver.

Sophie interrupts my search, "I see a restroom, and I'm going."

I roll my eyes, but then remember that we're all on our periods, with no end in sight and only the supplies I grabbed from the prison.

Situated above the restroom door is the iconic symbol for women, glowing softly inside a small rectangle about the size of a supper plate.

I follow Sophie toward the restroom. Mom's at my heels, and Tiff brings up the rear. My hands are filled with the menstrual cleansers, and I can't hit the lever for the restroom.

Sophie sees me fumbling and pushes open the door. She steps aside, holding it open. When we're all through, Tiff turns the thumb bolt to the locked position.

"Holy crap, that was awful," she comments. Her face is beat to a pulp. Her cheekbone is bruised, and one eye swollen half-shut. The visible slit of hazel iris is bright and pissed.

"Where are all the people?" I ask.

Mom looks at the solitary window. Textured glass obscures the view, and the light has grown dim since we came to the bathroom. "I imagine that the work day is through, and everyone's gone home."

"That'd be a lucky slice of timing," Tiff says, eyes traveling the generous-sized bathroom. There are six stalls, and like in our world, all the materials appear to be recycled.

Sophie is already at a sink basin, rummaging around in a screaming-hazard-orange handbag the size of a small suitcase. She sees us all staring. "What?"

I laugh.

Sophie raises her eyebrow above a perfectly aqua eye. "I never go anywhere without my purse."

Even other worlds, apparently.

How did that purse make it through the *blink*? How does she still *have* it? My questions must show on my face.

She gives a delicate snort, excavating horrible clothes one at time from the cavernous handbag. Sophie also has a smaller purse attached to her denim belt loop. "I have everything we need right here." Her voice is mildly triumphant.

"How come Brad and company didn't take that monstrosity?" Tiff asks, pointing to the ginormous handbag and giving the growing pile of clothes a suspicious review.

"They did, you sourpuss."

Tiff folds her arms, ignoring Sophie for the moment. "I could use a shot of tequila right now."

"That won't help us, Tiff," Mom says logically.

"Don't give a shit." Tiff slides a look my way. "Sorry about my potty mouth, Deegan. You're just gonna have to deal. I've been sober for about three seconds and feel like I just got jammed through a knothole then pulled back out."

The visual's terrible. "That's okay, Aunt Tiff."

"I hate feeling sharp," she mutters.

Mom puts her hand on Tiff's shoulder. "We need you to be. We're up to our eyeballs in this mess."

"I know, Jade." She grins. "Kinda like old times."

Mom sighs. "Not any of the ones I want to remember."

"Yeah, well, you were always okay in the damsel-in-distress role."

Mom puts her hands on her hips. "That's not fair, Tiff."

Tiff shrugs. "I know your dad was the biggest dickhead who ever lived, and that made you gun shy, but all I'm saying is I can be hard. It's natural, and you're just…"

"Found it!" Sophie squeals while I think there might be people in the corridor now. Looking for us.

Bots. I remember the yawning mouths screaming at me when they found out I was paranormal. I wipe my hands off on my filthy denims.

Sophie holds up a small rectangular pack of cleansing wipes. Unreal.

"Cat got your tongue?" Sophie asks Tiff in a smug voice.

"Nope," Tiff says with a smirk. "For once, your bullshit is going to do something important."

Sophie sighs and hands us each a pair of paper-thin leggings and a handful of wipes. Once out of the package, the wipes begin to biodegrade after ten minutes of oxygen exposure.

"I can't believe this is happening to me," Tiff mumbles.

I ask, "Why do you have six pair of leggings in there, Sophie?"

She blushes.

We go silent.

"I was thinking—when I got the pulse that Jonesy was getting together with the old gang—"

"Don't tell me you were gonna hook up with his man-whoring ass?" Tiff asks subtly.

Gawd.

Sophie slaps Tiff with a hateful look. "I've never really gotten over Jonesy."

"He's been married twice!" Tiff huffs, crossing her arms as her hazel eyes flash. "How do you not get over that number?"

"Three," Sophie says under her breath.

"Oh, Soph," Mom says, smacking her forehead. "Not Jonesy. He's too messed up with relationships."

"I like Jonesy."

They all turn to stare my way.

"He's nice to me," I say.

"You don't have to date him."

I make a face. "He's an old guy."

Sophie glares at me. "I'm viable. Brad said so. I can pop out a baby if I get a volunteer."

Oh, yes—*Brad's* the authority. *Please.* A guy barely a year and a half older than me.

"God, Sophie," Tiff says, scrunching her nose.

Sophie's bright eyes slit on Aunt Tiff. "And you can't tell me *you* don't want to have a baby?"

Tiff's face goes soft. Her hazel gaze grows shiny. "Hell yes, I want to spit out a kid." Tiff turns away from us, swiping at her eyes.

"Clean your crotch up—all of ya—and toss these awesome extra pants on I had in case I stayed over at Jonesy's." Sophie waggles her eyebrows.

Her revelations give me pit sweat.

"That was super optimistic, Sophie." Mom eyes her skeptically.

"That's me. I'm a half-full-glass kinda girl." She winks.

I hand everyone a menstrual cleanser.

We each move into a stall and clean up, throwing our wrecked pants into the trash separator.

"What in the hell is this thing?" Tiff screeches from her stall.

"It's a menstrual cleanser, Aunt Tiff," I say, inserting the cup-like device into the forward part of my entrance.

"This is just *gross*. I want my tampon," Sophie laments.

"Listen, can a tampon last for half a day?" I ask logically. Who really knows if we can find the guys, and Pax can *blink* us back when we want. We need a longer-lasting solution.

"Deegan's right. Tampons are familiar, but really, they'll need to be changed frequently, and then we're right back to a mess."

"A gross *embarrassing* mess," I emphasize. My words are greeted by silence.

"Fine," Tiff grumps.

We exit the stalls, and Tiff glares at Sophie.

"What?" she asks innocently, but her voice is filled with laughter.

"You gave me the lamest leggings on purpose."

We look at Tiff's leggings. They're a flaming-red-and-black zebra print.

I put my hand over my mouth. The red flames sparkle, too. I couldn't have selected anything *less* Aunt Tiff if I tried.

"And I look like I'm packing shit in the back!" she half-shouts, and pivots, grabbing some excess material at her butt region.

We all stare at Sophie's ample rear end, then at Tiff's little tiny one.

"They're clean, at least," I offer, getting a class-A crooked mouth. You know the kind, where it's super inappropriate to laugh, but managing not to is impossible. Like at funerals. Church. A job interview. Seems to be a Hart Family Problem.

I glance down at my leggings, which are shimmering black with pink polka-dots. Not my choice, but it's okay.

Mom's are hot pink with red lips. Super bad. "Thanks, Sophie." Mom smiles.

Mom's always so gracious about everything.

I'm grateful that I was able to ditch my grodie denims and wear something clean. I tell her thanks, too.

We look at Tiff.

"No, I look stupid." She crosses her arms, and so does Sophie.

Stand-off.

They have a staring match.

"Fine!" Tiff says, huffing to the main bathroom door and tearing it open.

I guess I won't have blood crotch to deal with. That's an upside.

There's a man who looms into the open doorway.

I have a second to realize he's wearing a cowboy hat before that familiar feeling spreads over me. The same one that I get around Uncle John.

Shit, this guy's a Null.

Tiff doesn't worry too much about the finer points and punches him in the nose.

There's a dull crunch.

"Take that, peckerwood!" Tiff shouts and steps over him.

His hand snakes out and grabs her ankle. Down, she goes, a blur of black-and-red zebra stripes.

Here we go.

⁙

Cowboy

I survey the deserted hallway and note the time— straight-up six o'clock.

The cyborgs are deactivated, recharging for the mundane activities of the next day. I stride past where they're stored and notice the softly glowing chests of their semi-hibernation state.

The other world doesn't employ cyborgs, from what the Thompson's have relayed. That might be another plus.

The door I need is to the left, and that pain in the ass, Kim, has been with the other-worlders long enough.

I don't want dickbag Brad up my ass because she got all sympathetic. Actually, Kim's not too bad—but I get pounded for anything she does wrong.

Sort of like babysitting but without the perks.

I trot down the steep cement stairs, which were installed long before using recycled materials became mandatory, and swing open the door.

Kim's not there.

And neither are the women. My heart surges up my throat, trying to knock its way out of my body.

There'll be hell to pay. Brad will have his daddy string me up by the gonads.

I look left then right before stepping forward. I trip and save my nose from getting broken by quick palms in front of my body. Still in push up style, I crank my head, glancing behind me to see what the fuck I tripped on.

Brad moans.

Oh fuck.

I swivel with my hands, tipping over, and lift one beat-up leather boot over the top of Brad's body, then the other.

I stand.

"Ron," Brad croaks, grabbing at his nuts with one hand and beseeching me with the other.

He's got a case of pancake nose with a chaser of dried blood. His mouth is bleeding, and there is a heel print of an old-fashioned sneaker at the side of his mouth.

I retreat a step. *This is bad.* Any way I turn the circumstance over in my head, I end up with my neck on the guillotine.

"What happened?" I ask, though that should be obvious.

The women somehow escaped, and Brad got his testes tapped. I feel a pang of sympathy. Almost. Unfortunately, Brad nipped whatever compassion I might have harbored in the bud just by being who he is.

"Zombies," he says, eyeballs bulging.

A stealthy noise to my immediate left alerts me.

I whirl as strong arms knock off my cowboy hat. *I love that hat.* Undead fuckers.

In automatic response, my Null ability washes over the room. Now that particular talent is no weapon against zombies.

Or their superior strength.

I dip down, snag the brim of my well-loved hat, and sprint back the way I came, leaving Brad to figure out the horde.

If he can.

I'll find the women, and maybe, if I'm really lucky, I'll get the hell out of this world where Brad can't follow me.

I don't think. Instead, I shut the door that's at the top of the staircase and use the key I've been assigned to engage the bolt. That won't hold determined zombies from coming after me, but as I look through the narrow rectangle of tempered glass, I watch Brad crawling toward the zombie that tried to give me a love squeeze.

I'm not hanging around to see what happens next.

Now, the women all began their cycles here. God, am I glad I'm a dude.

What'd be the first thing they would do after they were lucky enough to escape? My eyes shift in the direction of the bathroom.

Bingo.

I jog toward the door. How much trouble can it be to reason with them? The cute girl, Deegan, only appears to be a few years younger than I am, and the older women, well—they'll be more tame.

My hand hovers over the lever for the door entrance, and I hear a resounding click.

I frown, drawing my hand back as the thing swings wide, almost beaning me in the head.

There stands the skinniest one. Dark-hazel eyes peg me, one half closed. That gaze widens, and she punches me.

She's just a girl, I tell myself. But *the girl* busts my nose. Then she nails me in the fucking nuts.

I fold like a broken chair and mewl, breath wheezing through my tight esophagus.

I grab at her ankle, and she begins to topple.

As usual, easy just turned complicated.

Then I puke.

Perfect.

14

Deegan

"Oof!" I stumble into Tiff as she lays out the Null. "Aunt Tiff, he's down!"

"Shh!" Mom's eyes dive from left to right.

"Cyborgs," the man at our feet gasps. "Not too loud, or they're gonna wake up."

Gooseflesh has its way with me, crawling over every surface of my body.

Tiff whips her head from side to side then plops down on the Null, straddling him. Air leaves him in a harsh whoosh of breath. "Where, stud?" Stiff knuckles are poised above his exposed throat.

The Null blinks, gasping, "Everywhere." He looks her over, eyes staying on her crazy pants the longest.

Tiff scowls. "Don't even think about saying anything, cowboy."

"Hurting too bad to care about your lack of fashion sense, darlin'."

Oh my God.

Tiff shifts her weight, and he groans. "Where's that *bitch*, Brad?"

The Null inhales deeply then lets it out with a wince, still eyeing her hovering knuckles. "I'm not going to hurt you guys. Can you—" He looks at her for an awkward space of seconds. "Get off me?"

Tiff shakes her head. "Surprise was my advantage. I let you up, and you'll clobber me with your big ass."

His face reddens, his eyes shifting to mine.

The irises are a beautiful amber. I know this because the last of the dying sunlight strikes a wedge of pale, ambient light across his face, lighting them like soft lamps.

I realize this guy isn't that much older than I am. "Hey, Aunt Tiff?"

She doesn't look at me, keeping her eyes trained on the Null. "Yeah."

I hide a small smile by biting my lip. "Let him up, I don't think he's trying to hurt us."

Tiff's hazel eyes become slits. "Birds of a feather and all that happy ho-ho shit."

He sighs. "Listen, I'm not in any position to hurt anyone. Right now, I want to crawl off in a corner and lick my considerable wounds."

Tiff smirks. "Okay, big fella." She smacks him on his chest, and he grunts. "Next time, don't grab a girl that just socked ya in the schnoz and the nutsack. Doofus move."

"Doofus?" He quirks an eyebrow, clearly puzzled by the term.

"Tiff-speak," I translate a little helplessly.

The Null gives me a grateful look. "Okay."

Then Tiff is standing, and he rolls over, moving to his hands and knees. He spits on the ground by his pool of vomit and takes a few seconds to fortify himself before standing up.

He's tall and well-built. Not monstrous like Mitchell (not that I'm actively comparing) but lean and muscular.

Of course, everyone seems tall to me, but this guy is at least six-feet, two. His hair is a honey color, like his eyes, and falls in disarray every time he twitches his head, like he needs a perpetual haircut. The deep dimple at the exact center of his chin looks like a crater.

He managed to keep the vomit off his clothes—and they're an interesting mix. *Except I can't be interested.*

We need to get my family. And Mitchell.

The Null limps to the wall and leans his palms against it, taking quick swallows.

"My brother can fix you," I offer, feeling kind of bad about the Tiff-battering.

He swings his head in my direction. "My name's Ron."

"Hey," I say.

Sophie, Tiff, and Mom are silent.

He jerks his chin in their direction. "I know, I'm the enemy. But actually, I have a favor to ask."

"Careful what ya wish for," Tiff comments in a dry voice. She produces a piece of gum from I-don't-know-where, stuffing it in her mouth. Gum is gross. Never understood wanting to have something in your mouth you're not going to actually eat or drink. Yuck.

She's an expert, though, rolling the disgusting blob around in her mouth then blowing a big bubble that only allows her eyes to peek over the top of the neon-green growing ball.

"Don't pop that," Ron squeezes out, barely managing to stay upright.

"Damn." Tiff stabs the huge bubble with a finger and sucks the entire wad into her mouth.

Eew.

"I need to get out of here," Ron says, clearly as repulsed by Aunt Tiff's habit as I am.

Tiff snorts.

"I don't think that's possible. I guess we're grateful you didn't attack us, but this is the most inhospitable place we've ever traveled." Mom says.

"Amen," Sophie chimes in.

Ron's whiskey-colored eyes narrow on mine.

"It's pretty bad. With the zombie whorehouses and the Brad of my world with unlimited power here?" I shrug.

His eyebrows yank together, and he grimaces as he crosses his arms in front of him. "That's *why* I want out. I'm viable because I can control the few paranormals who escaped the camps—"

I get a bad feeling. "Camps?" I whisper.

"You know your history?" Ron asks, eyes sharp.

I shift my weight. "Yes—the history of *my* world."

"Well, there was this nutjob named Heinrich. German zealot type from the twentieth who thought it was a cool idea to wipe out everyone who was Caucasian."

I blink. *Hitler.* He means this world's Hitler.

"You got that wrong, friend," Sophie says, crossing her arms below her generous-sized breasts and creating a push-up-bra effect. "Hitler hated *everyone* of color. Had a real hard-on against Jewish people."

Ron's face screws into a frown. "I said Heinrich."

They stare at each other, then Sophie lifts her shoulders in an exaggerated shrug. "So you're saying in this world, being white is not cool?"

Ron chuckles. "Fair skin and eyes are not the ideal here. Caucasian people don't age well, aren't athletic, can't sing or dance or perform with the aptitude of people of color. So no, we're just around because we're part of the human race. Tolerated. Sometimes we get lucky, and a savant will crop up." He shrugs.

We stare at him, open-mouthed. Maybe the worlds aren't as parallel as we'd assumed.

"What?" he asks, his warm eyes shifting to the others then finally back to me.

"Things are very equal now, but there was a time—nearly a hundred years ago now—that the Caucasians"—I sort of stumble over the word it's so odd on my tongue—"would not allow people of all colors to be together."

Ron waves away my comment, dismissing the differences with a palm swipe. "Anyway, the camps are for paranormals. It's the first time since Henrich's reign in the 1940s that there's been that kind of segregation."

Extermination? I wonder.

"So our worlds aren't completely parallel?" I ask, disquieted.

"What was your first clue?" Tiff says, restraining herself from smacking the gum. She slides me a look like she's saying, *"You're dumb."*

I scowl.

Ron pushes away from the wall, and Tiff tenses.

But I want answers. I guess four girls against one man is doable. Especially one who is Body here. "So what's happening?"

"In the camps?" Ron asks, fixing his hat and running a smoothing finger along the brim in a gesture that looks like he's done it a million times.

I nod.

"We don't have time for this," Tiff says in a flat voice. "I want to break the guys out and get the hell out of this freak show. Too many clowns, not enough circuses."

Ron gives her a look.

She meets his stare with one of her own. Unflinching.

"She always like this?" He jerks his jaw toward her.

Some of the color is returning to Ron's face, but his nose is crooked.

"Consistency is key," Tiff comments in a Sahara Desert voice.

One side of his mouth quirks. "What I'm saying is, when the camps close down and they're done running their torture, experiments, and killing squads on the paranormals, they won't need me. And I know a *lot* about Thompson Enterprises and a helluva lot about the Helix Strand."

Helix Strand. *Helix Complex,* my mind instantly translates. And on the heels of that realization is what he doesn't say. Why keep Ron the Null around when he's been witness to who's participated in who knows how many horrible things?

"Pax can decide if he wants to *blink* you back to our world, but I'll be honest, Ron." Mom looks up at him, seeming to take his measure.

"Just touch him, Mom."

Ron frowns, giving Mom a speculative look. "What are you?" His eyes scan her face. Green eyes the color of Alaskan jade stare back wordlessly.

"Five-point Empath." Then her hand lands on his forearm, and there's not a lie that will stand against that kind of sensitivity. Thank God I'm not a schemer, or every idea I have would be naked before Mom.

In this world, she's practically omniscient.

Ron's eyes widen. "I can shut you down," he says softly, but he doesn't pull away.

"I know," she replies, "but I can't make a case for you if you're a liar and a criminal, now can I?" Her large emerald eyes collide with his amber ones.

Ron gently shakes his head. "No," he agrees quietly then cringes as Mom clearly skates over rough stuff. Really rough, judging by her expression.

When large tears brim then fall, I take her hand.

"No, Deegan. There are some things you can't unsee."

I let my hand fall.

"You were five when they took you." Mom's confident voice floats the corridor, striking me like a soft whip of horror mixed with awareness.

"Yeah." Ron's neck reddens.

"Gawd," Sophie mutters. "It's like the Graysheets all over again in this world, too. Shrouded and cloudy, but always muddling people's lives."

"Or taking them," Tiff adds.

From what Dad says, the covert government segment was much better at taking. Just taking.

Mom lifts her hand, flicks a tear off her cheek, and sucks a shaky breath. "It's awful here."

"Different awful?" Tiff asks, tossing her gum in a separator just outside the restroom door.

Mom's eyes skid in her direction. "Yeah. But somehow just as bad."

"Well?" Ron lifts golden-brown eyebrows that disappear briefly under the brim of his hat.

Mom slowly nods, giving a shock of black hair an irritated shove behind her ear. None of us really have any hair ties left. A lone one encircles my wrist. "I'll do my best, but the only thing they have is my word, because your actions…" She flips her palm out.

"They suck hind tit?" Tiff finishes in her oblique way.

Sophie laughs. "You are so *you*."

"Yeah, I'm gonna be *me*, and right now, that means you telling us where the men are."

Ron doesn't smile as he limps away, but he seems more at peace, at least for the short amount of time I've known him. "Follow me, ladies."

"Said the lion to the lamb," Tiff mutters. But she follows.

We all do.

If Mom thinks we can trust him, it'll have to be enough. Ron knows where the other half of my family is, and without Pax's ability to *blink*, all of us are trapped in this awful world.

We have a sanctioned reception waiting for us when we get back to our earth. And I'm scared about that unknown.

But what we do know about the bot world is worse. A future where Brad thinks he can breed a super race without recourse—that would mean his plans for my family would be really final. He can't have Dad, Mom, Gramps, and Pax around because they would never stop trying to safeguard me until their last breath.

And that's what I'm really afraid of. My abilities aren't the same on this world. I can't control the dead raised by others.

They feel me, but they're not mine.

And if they're not mine, then they're just zombies with criminal intent, superior strength, and awareness.

The right directive (or the wrong one) would render them uncontrollable by me or Pax.

But I did raise Mitchell. So I do have AftD here.

And Brad didn't seem to understand that the bot world criminal element might be mine and mine alone. That has potential. Not that I want to hang around and figure it out.

As we move down the hall, a pale-blue illumination seeps out beneath a door. The large pane of glass is the only untextured one in the hall.

Bots line the room like sardines. They appear to be sleeping. But my palms instantly dampen at the sight of the soulless bots in repose.

Tiff and I slow, gazing at the sleeping bots. "Creepers," she says in a soft voice.

Sophie plucks at Tiff's once-white T-shirt. "Come on, let's get to the guys and save the day."

Tiff tosses a last uneasy glance over her shoulder and walks quickly to where Mom and Ron are at the end of the hall.

I hesitate a moment longer. As I watch, bot eyeballs roll underneath opaque silver lids. Dreaming.

The bots dream.

The one directly in front of the door flutters its eyelids as though aware of being watched.

I gasp, turning on my heel, and quietly jog after the others.

What if the bot had woken up and seen an AftD-*blinking*-Manipulator-other-worlder?

I know the answer to that.

Game over.

15

Paxton

We're all doing the incognito chuckle over Gramps getting his love on in the bot world with Brad's twentieth cousin, or whatever the blue hell Kim is, when Dad opens the door and the cowboy Null walks inside.

Well hell…

His powers wash over me immediately. Actually, it's like being smacked in the face with an ice cold bucket of water.

Dad moves forward, and I expect him to karate chop the cowboy's ass or something—then Tiff moves around him.

"Hold up, Hart!" she barks.

Dad sort of tumbles in motion, slapping his hand on the doorjamb instead of the guy's Adam's apple.

"I'm Ron," Null Dude says.

Introductions are so overrated. I want to *blink* us all out of here when the girls conveniently pour through the door behind Null and Tiff.

No time like the present.

"We don't have a lot of time," Ron says, like it's an original thought.

"Yeah. I sort of stomped on millimeter boy's penis." Aunt Tiff snaps a bubble, and the guys grimace.

Mom goes right to Dad, and he scoops her against him. "Jade." He steps back, scanning her form thoroughly. "You're a sight for sore eyes."

She nods, tears streaming. Mom's always been pretty emotional.

"What's going on here, Tiff?" John asks, cautiously striding forward, taking inventory of her injuries while giving Ron a once-over.

"I want to go with," the Null says, holding up his palms like he's waving a white flag of surrender.

Gramps snorts.

This is our life.

Kim says, "You are in the Thompsons' pocket, Ron." Her eyes accuse.

I keep my fat mouth shut. Lots of info needing to be conveyed without me blabbing my two cents worth.

He nods, and I breathe easier when I catch sight of Dee coming through the door, followed by Sophie.

"Great, let's get the hell out of here."

Dad looks at me, his expression tight.

"Dad, you look constipated."

Tiff barks a laugh.

"Pax, I don't think we can just *blink* our way out of this."

Why not?

Gramps says, "I see you're not getting the bigger picture, Pax. The goon squad in our world will have one helluva a reception waiting for us." He cups his hand around the tip of a cigarette and lights it.

Gramps manufactured cigarettes here?

He squints at me through the smoke. "Unless you can coordinate latitude and longitude?"

I shake my head. *No way.* I don't have even close to that kind of finesse with *blinking.* Hell, I was lucky to get us back here. I look around our dismal cells and healing injuries.

Maybe not lucky...

Gramps watches my facial expressions. Seemingly satisfied he got the answer he expected, he turns to the Null. "You're the bright one who stormed in here rabbiting on about catching our tailwind." Gramps gives Ron a pointed look then tips his head back and shoots out a stream of smoke.

"Let's get out of the prison," Mitch says, his hands already on my sister's shoulders.

Makes me pissed. But I console myself with the fact he would literally give his left nut to protect her. So fuck it. For now.

"I agree with him," Kim says. "We're trapped in here if Brad can get help. The cyborgs are hibernating, but he can override that directive within this building."

I look to Dee, and she shivers. What cyborgs? Are there bots inside where we're being held right now? *Here?*

Not good.

"Smooth plan, my man." Jonesy heads for the door.

"Restrain your enthusiasm, Jonesy," Clyde says thoughtfully.

"What happened to Clyde?" Tiff asks.

His skin is falling off his face like peeling wallpaper. It's lost all color and has the tonal quality of fresh ash.

"Bobbi and Caleb are the only two who can arrest my degradation."

We all look at Clyde.

Looks like fresh grave to me.

"Sorry, Clyde," Dad says, his face a tight mask of guilt, helpless to put Clyde back in style because he has no AftD in this world.

Clyde spreads his hands wide, and the tip of one finger glances off the bar of his cell.

A small nub of flesh drops off the tip, rolling like a small gray pea that's been sheared off, somersaulting in tiny stuttering revolutions toward a center drain in the floor.

We mark the progress of the amputated fingertip as it falls through the pockmarked metal, into the running sewer below.

"That's truly awful," Sophie remarks.

Sophie's concern is over purses, shoes, and fashion but she might finally be getting the important points.

Speaking of. My eyes travel over the fugly leggings on everyone.

I guess it beats bleeding out. I take a second gander. *Barely.*

"That's unfortunate," Clyde comments, still staring after his lost fingertip. A tooth drops out of his mouth, following the path of the fingertip.

"Okay," Mom says, heading to the door and dragging Dad behind her. "Let's get out of here."

"What about?" I jerk a thumb toward Ron.

I hate a guy when I can't see his eyes. And this guy's ten-gallon hat shadows his stare.

"I don't think he can be trusted," Kim says, giving him the woman stink eye. (Yeah, that's different than the male version.)

"That's settled then," Gramps says.

Ron narrows his eyes on the two. "I get it. You want to bone Kim, so now it's her word against mine. The *Thompson* relative." He nods vigorously. "I see how it is. Or did you forget that little familial factoid when you were being led around by the little head?"

Oh shit.

Gramps jabs him in the face with a nicely executed uppercut. No warning. No words. Just pow.

Nice.

"Argh!" Ron staggers back, spraying blood from between his fingers as he covers his nose.

Sophie gives a little cry, covering her mouth. "Mac!"

Gramps says indifferently, "Might need a little lesson in manners."

"We can't go back yet," Tiff says, tossing a disinterested glance at the bleeding Null before turning her attention to me.

Huh. I glance around our prison. "Let's vacate, then talk." Kim had a point about there being one exit and the possibility of Brad showing up with reinforcements. Not a great defensive position. More like a juggernaut.

Jonesy points at me, "Good call, Hart spawn."

Mom's face goes sour.

Jonesy sees her expression and guffaws.

We traipse up the stairs. Aside from our footsteps, Ron's breathing through his mouth like a tortured duck is the only noise.

Kim is second behind Jonesy as we exit the top of the landing.

Nighttime is here, and I instinctively *blink*, my second eyelid descending seamlessly. I look to Dee, and she's using hers too.

I see fifty-year-old grime embedded in the sick-looking diamond floor.

I see blood that's been bleached.

Dee and I exchange a glance. Dust motes float between us like a distracting opaque moving blanket.

This building wasn't always used for what it is right now.

All the women wearing shitty pants physically hurts my enhanced sight. *That reminds me.* "You guys get the menstrual thing figured out?"

Gramps frowns, looking like he a swallowed a turtle. Whole. "In my day—"

"Mine, as well," Clyde interjects smoothly.

"Yeah," Tiff glances at Clyde with barely contained impatience. "We've got bigger fish to fry than whether or not we're talking about periods." She rolls her eyes.

"Like standing out in the middle of this hall, waiting to be discovered," Sophie adds.

Good point.

Mitch stays close to Dee but says, "It's safer here than out there. There isn't anybody working at night, it's after hours, and the bots have gone night-night."

Night-night? Clown. "Are ya making a funny, Mitch?"

Dee wrinkles her nose, moving closer to steroid zombie. "Pax, cut it out."

"Kids." We get a Primo Mom glare.

"Yeah, *kids.* Not helpful." Tiff turns her attention to me again. "So like I'm saying, we can conceive here in this world. But not in ours."

I swear Uncle John stops breathing, and Dee appears to be catching her breaths one at a time.

The implication nails me between the eyes. "You mean, you want to stay here long enough to… *disgusting.* I can't say the words."

We're discussing my Mom—Sister.

Never fear, Gramps is all about The Awkward. "I appreciate that you want children, Tiff—"

"You have no idea how much, Mac," John says in a quiet voice.

I mentally cringe. I guess we're *doing this.*

Gramps scrubs his face then pats down his pocket for a cigarette.

"What's going on?" Kim asks the women.

"Women aren't fertile in our world," John replies.

"Oh, you appear to believe that's a terrible fate, but what real need do you have for children anyway?" she asks matter-of-factly, searching the women's faces, which begin to darken seconds after her question.

Gramps and Jonesy beam.

Sophie punches Jonesy in the arm, and he yowls like a cat slipping on a wet roof.

"Shh," Ron the Null says. But it comes out like *shlurp* or something because his nose has been reduced to a tenderized lump of hamburger on his face. "The bots."

Larh bawts is what I hear.

"I already broke his nose once," Tiff says offhandedly. *God…*

John wastes a glance at Ron, a smile hovering over his lips. "That's my hellion."

Oh boy.

"Let's stay at the point," Dad says, staring directly at Tiff. "You want us to remain here, until you can have sex with John, in the hopes that you can get pregnant?" His dark eyebrows arch.

Tiff tilts her head for a second, appearing to ponder Dad's words. "You got it, Hart. A little wham-bam, thank you, ma'am, oughtta do the trick."

Uncle John turns beat red, like an overripe tomato. It's not a good look, but it earns a smile from Mom, who dips her chin to hide her expression.

"I don't want to stay here," Dee says in a thin voice.

Gramps pegs his hands on his hips. "Don't know if Tiff's plan is in the best interests of the group—hanging around in this surly world, hoping for compassion." Gramps gives a sharp grunt then lights up again. The ember at the tip of his cigarette winks like a bloated firefly then dies back.

"There isn't any," Kim says with such a straight face, it's funny.

But nobody laughs.

Gramps flips a palm toward Kim, sending a spiral of smoke spinning and floating toward the high ceiling inside the corridor. "What she said."

"I want a baby," Sophie says like a bomb detonation. Her words ring in the strange acoustics of the hallway. Though she spoke quietly, it seems to echo down the hall and come back to us like a stealth attack.

"Whew," Jonesy says, pretending to wipe sweat from his brow, "I thought you were going to say something really important like: I want to go back to our world where it's *safe*." Jonesy glares at Sophie.

She glares right back.

"I cannot believe that procreation is being discussed instead of our hasty retreat to the evils we know," Clyde says, straightening.

Another tooth falls. The sound of it clinking back down the stairs is swallowed by the sudden silence.

We gotta get out of here.

"Maybe you guys will still get pregnant after you get back?" Dee says uncertainly. "Like a delayed effect?"

Doubt it, my mind sings, but I don't say. I'm pretty sure the fertility effect is bot-world-only. Suck-ass irony.

Mom puts her hands on her hips. "I'm almost forty-two years old. I think I'd cry for a month if I found out I was pregnant now." Her eyes move first to Sophie then Tiff. "Why would you choose to be pregnant at our age?" Then Mom looks at Dee. "And I'd cry enough for two if you were pregnant."

Dad looks like he wants to toss chunks. Thinking about Dee boinking some dude is *so* not on the mental contemplation list. Disgusting.

Dad and I simultaneously glare at Mitch.

He glares right back, emitting a low-level hiss.

Clyde cocks a brow, the ghost of a smile shadowing his decaying lips.

Mitch's hands fist, and I notice for the first time that he's got a little black around the mouth. Dee's usually better than that.

"I'm not going to throw Deegan down and ravish her, Hart assholes." His eyes are straight razors in his face.

Gramps smacks his palm to his forehead, and ten centimeters of ash float to the floor. He grinds his shoe over the top in a move so automatic, I know he's done it a thousand times.

Kim's face puckers at the nasty cig ash.

"When we go back, there *will* be sanction police." I set my gaze on Dee. "I'm sorry, sis, but you zapped body parts." I shrug. That's just the kind of shit that gets noticed.

Dee's lower lip trembles, and shame floods her face.

I move on, though if we were alone, I would hug her. Her abilities are more fucked up, unpredictable, and wild than mine are. She got the shit end of the paranormal stick for sure. "If we stay here, I don't know if we can survive long enough for…" I wave my hand around, avoiding words like:

Sex. Fucking. Lovemaking.

Impregnation.

I shudder.

"Coitus?" Clyde offers, the promise of a shit-eating grin riding his face. Though in an effort to keep teeth in his mouth, he puts a lid on it.

Isn't he hilarious? Not.

Dad holds up a hand. "Thank you, Clyde."

Clyde inclines his head. "You are most welcome, Master."

Dad glares.

Clyde's grin bursts over his decayed face. And I notice holes where teeth should be.

At least someone has a sense of humor.

"There *are* no babies. If all of us can get pregnant, we should." Tiff looks at Mom, Dee, and Sophie.

Uh-huh. Hells no, sure as shit *not* Dee.

"I'm not an infant, Pax," Dee says, intuiting my internal rant perfectly.

Saying I'm conflicted doesn't cover it. My eyes move to Mitch. "I'm going to kill him if he lays a finger on you."

Mitch steps forward, trying to loom. (He's not half-bad at that, either.) "Listen, you asswipe—"

Gramps smirks.

"Dee is underage," Mitch states as though reciting a law.

He probably is—2010 law. But not a current one.

Jonesy swivels his hips, doing a parody of chopper dick. *Shit.*

"Do your civic duty—" He chuckles. "For the good of the world. Plus!" he yells, hips still rotating obscenely. "They won't touch a woman who's pregnant in our world. Too rare."

For once, Jonesy said something that is really smart.

The silence tells me he hit the nail on the head. If the women were to get pregnant, then our world could do nothing. Even if Dee *could* zap everybody's parts.

I get an image of the penises of all the Graysheets flying off into the ether, and an insane chuckle leaps out before I can stop it.

Gramps raises and eyebrow. "You gonna be okay?"

Not sure. I laugh again, and it sounds kind of like an aborted hiccup.

A new thought occurs, sobering me for the moment. The sanction police couldn't do anything to the men who were the fathers. There's a federal mandate. All life shall be preserved. That fed law went into effect after Zondorae's little potion fucked up procreation for the duration.

That takes Dee, Mom, Dad, Tiff, John, Sophie—I look to Jonesy, who is whistling tunelessly—and maybe Jonesy off the Kill List.

Lastly, I gaze at Mitch, and he scowls back at me.

He better not touch my sister. I don't care if we're desperate for population back home.

"Hey," the Null calls from behind me, "can you heal me, Kim?"

Ron the Null.

Hell no.

16

Deegan

"There's a lot more to the equation than some other-world nookie." Gramps cups his chin, and Kim, their healer-slash-jailor, smiles. This is so many shades of weird, I don't think we're on the same planet.

Oh yeah, *we're not*. I groan.

Dad slaps his forehead.

"For instance," Gramps goes on, seemingly oblivious to my parents' lack of enthusiasm with his need to explain, "we need grub, drink, and rest. Not in that order. I feel like I've been squirted through spin cycle."

Blank looks meet his words. Then it comes to me—those old-fashioned washing machine things. Dad told me they were still handwashing when he was my age. Seems beyond dumb now.

"We still use those here," Kim says.

Gramps's face whips to her. "God love ya."

She smiles again.

Hmm.

He snaps his fingers. "Can we get to your house easily?"

"Undetected," Uncle John adds.

Gramps scowls at John. "Right, big for britches."

John sighs. "Someone has to err on the side of logic, Mac."

"That's me—so illogical." Gramps's scowl turns to a glare that he directs at John.

I bristle. Gramps has single-handedly saved our skins. At least, that's how he would say it.

Everyone's just grouchy.

I could use some food. My stomach takes that opportunity to voice its emptiness.

Mitchell raises an eyebrow at the sound.

Gah. I hate being me. On my period, in the stupid bot world, talking about having sex to get pregnant.

In front of my parents.

Could anything epic and spectacular happen? Probably not.

"If I don't eventually shift planets, Brad will find me." Kim's serious enormous brown eyes move over the small knot of us.

She's kind of pretty in an old-girl, doe-eyed way. I look at Gramps. He thinks so. *Ick.*

"We call it *blinking*," Pax says.

Kim doesn't seem to care about the difference in terminology. "If I don't escape in a really permanent way, he'll make an example out of me, and Clem will allow it. They're very big on control."

I can tell. Brad was big on control in our world. Now we accidentally moved him to one where he and his tyrant dad can have unlimited dominance.

"Let's shelve the breeding commentary for the moment," Jonesy says, holding up a surprisingly pink palm in contrast with his dark-brown skin.

Sophie gives a disgruntled squeak, and he ignores her. "Mac's plan rocked. We head to Kim's hood and get some chow, drink beer." Jonesy gives a casual lift of his shoulder.

"No." Mom's flat voice echoes the stance of her crossed arms and tapping foot. She's hard to take seriously with the lips all over her legs.

Jonesy blows out an exasperated exhale. "Right. *I'll* drink beer." He waggles his brows. "And catch some shut-eye. After I've gotten sufficient beauty rest, I'm ready for the beat-down back home. You guys feel me?" He rubs the middle of a super-toned chest.

And I'm *underage?*

"I actually don't have beer," Kim mentions.

Jonesy frowns as though he'd never imagined she might lack beer. "Well, that blows. What about other booze?"

Kim's brows fold between her eyes.

"Jones," Dad pleads.

"Joy-sucks," Jonesy mutters.

"Joy-what?" Kim and Ron repeat (Ron's version is unintelligible).

"Where is your domicile?" Clyde asks smoothly.

"Is he always like that?" Mitchell asks quietly, giving a less-than-subtle glance in Jonesy's general direction.

I nod. "Always."

"Follow me," Kim says, trying to smile at Clyde and not quite managing.

Could be the smell.

I look closely at his gaping, nearly toothless mouth and peeling gray skin.

Or maybe it's the dead look.

We follow her, and Kim uses an actual key she retrieves from her small purse to unlock the door from the inside. I only know what the strangely-shaped metal key is because I actually paid attention to history, and my *Devices for Daily Living* pulse book was fascinating. The things everyone did to just exist seems like so *much*.

Once outside the building, I don't know about the others, but I feel lucky Brad didn't locate us while we were yakking about having babies and escaping, instead of actually getting out of there so any of that would even be possible.

Pax stands close to me, and we look out over the nightscape together. This is the part of my ability that he and I share. Both our second eyelids allow us to see everything in near-microscopic detail.

The moon is exactly half full, and that's really lucky for us because a full moon would be blinding with our night vision.

With a half moon, we see everything.

My eyes sweep left, and Pax's look right. After Brad took us prisoner, by poisoning us into a numbing coma, we didn't know how we got where we ended up. The guys had been beaten into submission, but the girls had gotten some kind of horse tranquilizer. I touch my neck, still feeling the scabbed over pinprick of that flying needle that nailed me.

I'd assumed we were being held in the thick of bot city or something because of all those legs sweeping past the semi-subterranean windows. But I'm wrong. We're in a rural location.

Dense forests are claustrophobic around the building where we stand on the highest step of at least twenty stairs, with narrow walkways circling the building.

Low sparkles appear on the treads of the steps like steel-colored diamonds mixed with ivory. *Granite,* I recognize.

Like gravestones.

That's an expensive material in our world. Pax and I slowly turn around to look at where we just came through.

Tall, gallery-height (illegal) wood doors stand three meters tall by two wide. Ornately carved with grapes and leaves, they appear to be very old. Original to the building, if I had to guess.

The building itself mimics Roman architecture, and I'm instantly transported to the world we just came from, where the Reflectives used mirrored surfaces to springboard everywhere. Like that jerk Ryan.

Fat fluted columns rise like spears to catch a marble gable-pitched hunk of roof that has cupids and grapes carved at its apex.

The sight should be awe-inspiring. But it's just creepy.

"Weird," Pax whispers.

Yeah, I answer him in my head.

There's a sign at the top, wedged between the cupids' distended bellies. It's worth a shudder.

"This used to be a church," Mitch says, breaking the silence like a hammer to glass.

Pax and I jump.

"Giver of Life," Gramps chortles. "No irony there."

"Yeah, those buttmunches were keeping us there and trying to torture and maim. Giver of Life, my ass," Tiff says, giving an indelicate sniff.

"There are no beliefs of any kind here. We have a completely neutral world." Kim's eyes skate over the words of the building dispassionately, then she looks away.

I follow her gaze.

Below us are a million twinkling lights.

Her version of Kent.

"If I use my transport, it'll be catalogued. Hardly anyone walks. Only bots."

"I saw people walking," I say, remembering all those restless feet streaming past the glass.

"Handlers." Kim gives a sad laugh.

Gramps puts a hand on her shoulder, and I notice how big it seems on her body.

"What's a handler?" Dad asks.

She lifts the shoulder where Gramps's hand rests. "It's perfunctory role, really."

"Per-what?" Jonesy bellows in what is his normal volume.

"Shh," Sophie says, and Ron makes a noise of fear in his throat.

We look at him.

"Cyborgs," he says like a slap.

"Yes," Kim agrees, eyes tight. "Anyway, a Handler is someone who manages one hundred bots. It was a failsafe measure implemented in the first part of the twenty-first to maintain human primary."

I'm not lost, but I don't like what I'm interpreting. My mind makes a bunch of leaps, and for one of the first times, I'm glad I'm a numbered IQ.

Time savings for understanding is great.

"So over time, what you're really saying is these bots have overtaken humankind in a matter of sheer numbers." I search everyone's faces, but before I can get feedback, Kim begins to walk, taking us and the conversation with her. "No one is producing kids anymore, and these bot things—"

"Cyborgs," Kim says.

"Yeah—cyborgs—are doing everything rudimentary for people. All the tasks that we do in my world are now being performed by them." I flip a palm in the broad direction of where all the lights sparkle a couple of kilometers away.

"There are no rudimentary disciplines left, so why make more people?" Clyde reiterates in his unique way.

And he's right. That's exactly it. All the simple stuff is getting done by a bot.

"The Handler is just supposed to assure Compliance within the cyborg community."

As soon as our toes enter the border of the forest, the darkness seeps toward us. Pax and I automatically move to flank Kim. We should be at the front of the pack. No one here will see better than we can. But we don't know where she lives.

"Assurance?" Mom asks in a quiet voice.

Kim nods, though I don't think anyone sees her, except my zombie.

I look just as Mitchell *blinks*. A second eyelid descends and he smiles. His teeth are very white in the dark.

The appearance of the eyelid startles me so much that I jump back. Attempting to counterbalance my fall, I succumb to gravity instead. I'm not known for my grace.

Mitchell reaches out to snatch me back, but I roll down the hill.

I travel, ass-over-tea-kettle, all the way down the slope. My heart beats against my ribs as I hurtle into a mound of something so brittle, it shatters when it breaks my fall.

Every piece of me instantly bruises, and I lie there for a moment, gauging if maybe I'm not completely broken, listening to everyone crash through the brush after me.

I *blink*, my second eyelid retracting then descending. The moonbeams claw through the canopy like determined talons of bluish-silver light. I stare into the night sky that manages to peek through pine needles so dense, shape and form are stolen.

I wiggle my toes.

My zombie having the *blink* and what that could mean worms its way through my brain.

It's not possible for a zombie to take on the attributes of its AftD host.

But I saw that iridescent second skin descend over the bright blue of his eyes, making the irises into shrouded sapphires.

I sit up, pressing my palms to the ground on either side of my body.

I yelp, bringing up my left hand and a shard of something white and sharp has pierced the meatiest part of my palm. I pluck it out and toss the unidentified piece away from me.

Have to have Pax figure that newest wound out.

Everyone finally makes it down the embankment. My eyes roll over their expressions. Embarrassment seizes me for my klutzy spin in front of Mitchell. Relief pours through me because I'm not actually hurt.

Kim covers her mouth with both hands. Eyes like melted chocolate stare back uncomprehendingly.

I know Mitchell is brave. His feet make sounds like he's crushing crackers as he walks to me.

But I don't know how brave, until after he comes down and pulls me up by my armpits, and I see what I landed on.

What speared my hand.

Bones.

Bones of the dead lay in a littered graveyard without markers. Not sanctified, merely abandoned.

"What is this?" I whisper, rubbing my bleeding palm on the ugly borrowed leggings.

"The dead," Mitchell restates the obvious.

Like knows like, Dad always says.

But nothing had pinged on my undead radar. That just means I can't raise them. And everything on this planet is so screwy, it's hard to know why I didn't know I'd landed in a literal graveyard.

"I'd give my left nut for some AftD juice about now." Jonesy's eyes are sharp, taking in the uncountable number of dead.

The sea of bones spread endlessly, no shore in sight.

"But hunger calls," Jonesy says, looking around for voices of assent.

I have no voice; my stomach has quieted. There's something wrong with these dead.

Pax and I look at each other. Tiff's tears solidify the sight. She sinks to her haunches and reaches out. She snatches her hand away then reaches out again and, with a sucking inhale, picks up a skull.

The head is so tiny, it barely fits inside her palm.

"Babies," she whispers. "It's not that you guys don't *want* babies." She looks an accusation Kim's way, "It's that when ya do—somebody is killing them all."

Tiff carefully sets the fragile skull on top of so many others and cups her elbows, silent tears streaming down her face. "There's not enough booze on all the planets for *this*."

The monstrous silence between us eats up the oxygen, making it hard to breathe.

"It's those fucking bots," Gramps says, giving Kim a hard look.

I don't believe for one second that Kim's the bad guy here. I think this world is just that bad. And I don't think I've ever heard Gramps drop an F-bomb. From the look of it, neither has Pax. This infanticide is worth an F-bomb. Or a hundred.

The women are crying.

Mitch turns my face to his, and his hand comes away wet.

There's some horrors you can never unthink, never unfeel.

Never unremember.

But wanting to undo what's happened burns into a person's very soul.

"I can't raise them," Pax says into the stillness of our witness.

I peek from Mitchell's embrace, his large hand cupping my head like he'll never let go.

"Why?" I ask.

"I can't stomach it," he admits. "It's too horrible, even for an AftD."

"I want answers," John says.

Jonesy shudders for all of us. "Not me. This is awful and creepy and just wrong. But it's not our world. I'm starving, and I want to get out of here before we're added to the skull heap." Jonesy jerks a thumb at the dead, eyes sweeping the dark for bots or some other threat.

Kinda cold.

Then Tiff launches at him like a leaping cat, claws and teeth extended.

"Ah!" he wails, trying to cover his head as Tiff pounds him. "Fuck me!"

"Tiff!" John yells, striding over there. Easier said than done when a person is attempting to avoid stepping on infant skeletons.

"Don't you see, you selfish prick!" Hit. Smack. Kick. "They're *people*, moron!"

Jonesy grabs her arms and shakes her. Her light-brown hair hits him in the face twice before he stops. "I know it, you insane bitch!" His eyes leap at her—all of us. "But you can't save them, Tiff. Ya can't. Ya can't save them all."

Tiff collapses against Jonesy, and he holds her, stroking her back. "Ya can't save them, girl. Even if you wanna be everyone's baby mama, you can't." He pats her awkwardly. "It's okay, Tiff."

"I hate you," she sniffles, wrapping her arms around him.

John finally gets there, and Jonesy flips him off behind her back and smiles. "I love you, you stupid twit."

"I love you, too, Jones."

We stay for a little while longer. When we finally move on, we're heavier than we were before.

Grief will do that.

17

Gramps

Precious minutes were wasted yammering on about the reality of the bot world killing babies.

Of course they are.

Bots don't have souls. That's why they call it *artificial life*, candy asses. Cyber technology evolves. It's not meant to remain static. The very technology is fashioned to grow and become more.

Can anyone say Matrix?

Forget it. No one remembers the good old days when implausible science fiction was bullshit entertainment, and that was the extent of it. Pass me the popcorn, guys.

I scan the depths of the forest, wishing for the grandkids' special eyelids. Then I think better of it. *Nah.* What a trumped-up hassle that would be.

Kim's a cutie. Too bad she's from this world. Maybe she can be redeemed if she gets *blinked* to our world. That's leaping from the frying pan to the fire, though. Deedie's made a mess of things back home, too. Feels like the four walls of the box we've landed in are closing in.

And the answer to all the womenfolk getting knocked up to avoid sanctions seems like a really bad plan.

I eyeball Deedie.

A really bad plan. If I was a betting man, I would say Pax and Caleb aren't keen on her doing the hanky-panky between the sheets. Especially with Mitch.

There must be another way.

But right now, as horrible as it sounds, I'm with Jonesy. We need to skip out on this little parade and get some food, or we'll all be worthless. Those bag of bolts might run on fuel (and don't ask me what kind, because hell if I know). But I'm of the human variety, so I'll take regular meat and potatoes.

And a good dark beer. Yeah, that'd go down smooth right about now.

"Mac!" Jonesy says.

"Huh?" I turn to look at him, slide my jaw back and forth, and note that Kim doesn't have as much healing juice as Pax. Thing goddamned throbs like a tooth begging to be pulled.

"I called your name forty-one times."

I crack a smile. That damn kid. Consistent as the sun rising. *A consistent pain in my ass.*

"We're getting together a vote."

I search out the guys. John and Caleb still seem solid. And Clyde—hell, he's the Rock of Gibraltar.

The girls look shaken. Tiff, the toughest broad I've ever met, looks the worse for wear. Poor thing, fresh off the sauce and wanting kids so bad, she can taste it.

John has an arm around her shoulders, and Jonesy, the clod, has a hand on her other shoulder. He's a good kid, even if socially, he massacres everyone around him.

Jonesy moves back to the vote topic. "We go to Kim's and descend like locusts on whatever she has."

Sounds like a class-A Jonesy scheme.

I spare Kim a glance and she gives the thumbs-up. Now there's a trooper. *And she can kiss.* Thinking about the stolen moment gives me the second boner of the evening, and I beat it down by thinking about my great-granddaughter having sex with Mitch.

Limp noodle goes into immediate effect.

"Can't believe there'd be a need to vote on this." I put my hands on my hips, hating the grit of all that we've been through. I have a layer of filth plastered all over me. What I would do for a shower.

Jonesy's eyebrow rises. "Or, we *blink* back right now. Take our chances. Get the hell out of Murder World."

Name change suits the place. I pat my shirt pocket, find an empty carton where fine cigarettes used to reside, and glower.

Don't like *blinking* back in the present one little bit. The group's fatigued. Hungry. Pissed.

The sanction screwballs are waiting with some real firepower there in our home world.

Probably have a hundred five-point Nulls lounging around.

All because Deedie spun off those goons' body parts like she was throwing a Frisbee.

I chuckle.

Everyone frowns.

I guess my internal monologue is not transparent enough. Probably a good thing. Don't know if folks would understand my brand of humor. But that's the beauty—they don't have to for me to get a laugh. Sometimes humor is all that's left.

I glance over at Clyde. He might understand. He being of a similar ilk and a relation and all.

Gotta figure that out when we're not ass deep in alligators.

I let my hand fall to my side, feeling the ghost of my cigarette like a weight. "We should go to Kim's. I don't like Pax *blinking* the gang back without adequate stores. When was the last time we slept—or ate?"

Nobody knows. Vacant expressions and drooping eyelids greet my old eyes. Thanks to the rejuvenation, I no longer need reading glasses. I dig being eight-five and looking fifty. Don't want to get too young, though.

I was an asshole back in the day.

"Thoughts?" I spread my hands.

Jonesy opens his mouth, and Sophie says, "Quiet, Jonesy, we all know your belly calls."

In silent consensus, we had all moved carefully out of the mass grave of infants and back to the top of the ravine.

None of us speak about Tiff's meltdown.

Deedie broke her wrist and got a big lump on her noggin for her trouble, along with a macabre stabbing from a broken bone.

That girl could always trip over her own feet. But Pax set the mess of her injuries to rights.

I give a critical eyeball to Pax, who's looking so tired, his skin is ashen. We need rest. The boy simply can't heal everyone then *blink* us all back.

We might lose more people.

Like we did with Bry Weller and Archer. Where in the seven shades of hell did they run off to?

Later.

I look around at the rag-tag mess of family and friends. "Let's just stay on task, get to Kim's house and regroup."

"Can I say something?" Ron asks, wheezing exhaustively through his mouth.

I kind of feel bad about his mashed nose, but the man has a mouth that begs for slapping. *Talking about my dick and that. Hmm.*

"May I cuff him?" Clyde inches closer.

Ron the Null flinches.

I chuckle. I liked him better when he was just trotting along behind us like a puppy. We sure pick up a lot of strays. My eyes trail over Kim. Some I like.

"No ear cuffs, Clyde." Caleb sounds weary.

Morose group.

"Lead on," I say to Kim.

She surprises me by taking my hand. "I'm so glad I saved you."

That gets my dander up. "I would have worked out a plan." I'm not ruffled that a woman thinks I needed saving. At all.

She winks. "Uh-huh."

Tart.

The crowd quiets, silently walking behind us, though the grandkids with their astute sight are flanking me and Kim.

Somehow, I can't shake the feeling that danger is waiting for us. This world. Our world.

Danger waits.

❧

Pax slaps a palm on the last big tree before forestland breaks to cityscape.

"What do you call this city?" I ask, thinking it looks eerily like Kent from back home.

"Kent," Kim says.

Chicken skin breaks out, and I rub my hands over my arms.

"What is it, Gramps?" Jade asks at my elbow.

I gaze down at her, see the ghost of Deedie hidden in those features, and raise my arm.

Jade's small hand encircles my bare skin.

Seconds slip by, and when she lifts her hand, I feel the absence of that all-knowing touch.

"You don't think we're out of danger?"

I shake my head, because I certainly can't shake the feeling of impending doom. "Got a feel for that kind of business."

"What kind of business?" Pax asks, forehead against the rough bark of the tree.

"The bad kind, son."

He turns his head, and dark bluish-gray eyes meet mine. I know their color but can't make it out in the deepest part of the night. He can see the flecks of gray swimming in mine. I know because he's told me.

Judging by how I feel, the old bod would love to be under the covers and toasty warm about now.

Instead, I find my old ass in another world, in a version of Kent that has a hundred bots to one human.

Swell.

Clyde's smell precedes him, and I wrinkle my nose.

"Apologies," he says, though the one word sounds garbled. Caleb has told me the mouth is the last to get nailed down and the first to go.

Zombie anecdotal facts. "Can't help the reek, I suppose."

"Too true," Clyde says, swiping his hand against some hanging skin and flicking it off his fingers.

The glob of flesh lands against the tree beside us, and the flap of skin sticks like a grotesque gory flag against the bark.

"That is so gross," Sophie says.

It is, but I've seen worse. Hell, back in the Gulf War, I saw stuff that I could never unsee. A little bit of cadaver flesh flying around isn't going to get me squeamish.

"I live there," Kim says, dropping my hand to point.

I follow the direction of her finger.

A narrow strip of older brick buildings are railroad tracks in their design, so close together that the alley separating them could hardly accommodate a fossil fuel car.

Thinking it makes me miss the Camaro. Those sanction fellas better not have any ideas about running through my place. *Chumps.*

Everyone looks to the sky.

No hover transport. Huh. "Where's the transport?" I ask.

"Curfew," Kim replies.

Of course, the tyrant bots are all over control. Probably make it sound plausible and justified to the human populace. I'm naturally suspicious, so to me, it stinks like a skunk.

I survey the group, seeing everyone is more or less ready, and a somber Tiff gives me a jerking nod. "Let's go."

"Wait," Kim says, her hand floating to my arm. Warming it. She turns around, her back to the waiting city, facing everyone. "There is a strict curfew in effect. That means that if we trip one of the cyborg wires, they will make us Compliant."

What?

"Don't like the sound of that," Pax replies slowly.

"Me, either," Caleb agrees.

"They sound a lot like the Sanction Police." Deedie gazes around the forest, like the bots will jump out of the ground. Robot zombies.

I laugh.

Everyone gives me strange looks. "Just thought of something. No worries," I say, using an ancient expression.

Caleb smiles because he's always had a bit of a challenge with controlling his urge to laugh. I just let it rip.

"So how do we avoid the bot booby traps?" Jonesy asks, getting to the crux of it.

"I see them," Pax says in a soft voice.

"Me, too," Deedie echoes.

I look where they're looking. Don't see squat.

"That's not possible. They're infrared."

Mitch's eyes travel the first half block or so of the edge of the city. "It's a graph of some kind. We'll have to walk through it like a maze."

Deedie looks down, and I sharpen right up at Mitch.

"What in the hell is going on here, Deegan?" Caleb asks.

"Now don't go too hard on her," I begin. The poor kids can't help their genetic deck of cards they got dealt.

Deedie's bottom lip trembles. "I was hoping he'd stop *blinking*, Dad."

Oh *boy*.

"What is it, baby?" Jade asks, pushing all the snarled dark hair behind Deedie's ear. Half of her thick long hair is in a braid, and the rest a mess. Leaves and twigs are sticking out of it from the cartwheels she did down the hill.

Mitch plucks a few pieces of forest debris from her hair like a devoted chimp. His face turns to mine.

He *blinks*, and an eyelid descends. A second one.

This isn't good.

"I didn't mean to give him my *blink*."

"Oh, Caleb, this is dreadful."

"I didn't think anyone who was dead could take on the attributes of the AftD?" John states.

"Looks like Deegan's got all kinds of stuff she can do," Tiff says.

"Can he *blink*, or can he *blink*?" Pax asks.

"Ah—no. Don't want to see if Deegan's corpse-boy can jettison us to some other place even more screwed up than this one."

Hate to say it, but for once, I agree with Jonesy.

"I'm not going to do anything like that. I said there's a grid in a graph-like pattern. I can see it, and Deegan and Pax can see it." He looks at each one of us. "I say we split up, everyone hold the back of everyone else, and we move through the grid. Between the three of us, we should navigate the pattern easily."

Pax sighs, ripping a hand through his hair. "Fine. But I'm beat."

We all are.

"I don't know what this *blinking* thing is precisely, but it better work. None of us want to become Compliant." Kim's eyes are too wide in her pale face.

"What's 'compliant' exactly?" Deedie asks.

"Have you heard of the lobotomies given in the early twentieth?" Kim's dark eyebrows arch.

Christ on a crutch.

18

Deegan

Fine drops of sweat cascade down between my shoulder blades, soaking the center of my already-filthy shirt.

And my menstrual cleanser is nearly full.

Sophie's fingers through my shirt like a bad feeling I can't shake. I suck in air through my nose, trying to calm my shredded nerves.

Good luck with that.

I know that we've split the group to be fair to the three of us who have the enhanced vision because of the *blink*. I have the smallest number of people. Gramps is the caboose of my danger train.

I begin to tremble, and a lone drop of sweat slides from my temple to my jaw before falling to my shirt.

"Stop," I say, and everyone halts.

I turn to Mitch, who is about three meters to my right. Pax is exactly the same distance to my left.

Everyone's wide eyes look to me. It's not lost on any of us that we're literally walking through a mine field.

My head feels hot and weightless. "I think I'm going to be sick."

"No, Deegan," Pax says immediately. "You puke, and bodily crap's gonna get on the grid."

"She's exhausted," Mom says.

A scalding tear joins the sweat rolling down my face. "What if I trip?" I whisper.

Gramps's hand lands on my shoulder, breeching the distance between me and Sophie. "Listen to me, Deedie."

I zoom in on Gramps's voice and exhale, smelling my own sour breath. My stomach flips.

"I'm scared, Gramps."

He squeezes my shoulder hard enough for me to swallow a yelp. "You're a good girl. Shore up now, Deedie— we need you." He hesitates. "I promise you an ice cream when we get back home."

Sugar is illegal now. But Gramps has everything we can't have because of his holographic card that states his grandfathered status.

I smile, take in a breath, then let it out.

I can do this.

"You can do this, Deedie." Gramps echoes my thought, giving another one of his painful squeezes, and releases me.

Pax raises an inky eyebrow. "We gotta do this before light comes, Dee. If we don't, our sight will be back to normal, and we'll be as blind as them."

Aunt Tiff snorts. She's been so quiet since the baby skeletons that I'm glad to hear anything from her. Even if it's a pissed-off snort.

"Okay," I say, proud my voice doesn't shake.

I inch forward, sighting in on the dotted sharp red lines that run in a zig-zag pattern all around us.

Part of genius is innovation. My mind effortlessly finds the "holes" in the patterns, the "gaps" I can move between.

My zombie has the hardest time. Those voids in the grid are almost too narrow for a person as large as he is to pass through.

"I'm not so sure I don't want to take my chances here," Ron the Null mutters.

"Whatever. When we get out of gridland here, pal, you can take your chances with the bots," Gramps growls.

"*Blinking*? Zombies collecting trash? And what about all this nonsense about Pulse Tech? Your world sounds barely better than mine."

At least we're not baby killers.

"It's not nonsense," Sophie says in a lofty voice right behind me. "I don't have to use keys or handheld devices. We just *think* our communication needs, and poof! Done. And no zombie brothels, by the way."

Ron's irritated voice rants on, as he ignores the obvious issues of bot world, "Sounds like a great way for the government to keep tabs."

Nobody replies to that. We're so tense, we can hardly think, and discussing our messed up government history, the Graysheets, and all that's gone so wrong in our world isn't worth mentioning. Still, this world has worse problems than ours.

Gramps would think Ron's right, though. He won't allow the final pulse implantation that everyone gets when the cerebral cortex is fully formed after age twenty-five.

The implementation advancement wasn't without problems. Some subjects had implantation too early, resulting in some fried brains. Now the incomplete installation happens at five years, like a raw install. Everyone must be at least twenty-six and a half years to receive the complete Pulse chip.

I slow, and Sophie does the same behind me. My eyes travel the grid, and I see it collapse at the alley where Kim said she lives.

Okay. *Just three more meters.* I resume walking.

Pax uses his shoulder to wipe sweat from his forehead. First one side, then the other.

Mitchell doesn't sweat. Must be nice. Except the undead part.

We shuffle slowly to the end of the grid, where there's a solid line without breaks. It runs from the corner of one of the brick buildings all the way to the other.

"How do we get past this?" I ask, a lump of unshed tears seating itself in my throat. The line is chest height on me and has crosshatching from that point to the ground.

There's no way through.

Fear crawls up my throat like freed razor blades, spinning and slicing. I wipe my hands off on the scratchy polka dot pattern on my leggings.

"I can jump it then haul everyone over," Mitchell says, his gaze clearly traveling the same hurdle mine just did.

Gramps gives him a considering look, as do the other guys in the group. Except Pax and Dad. They know what zombies can do.

I look at Mitchell. His eyes meet mine. The expression in them simply says I'll be the very first person he hauls over.

That's okay by me. I'm scared to my marrow.

"Deegan first," Mom says unnecessarily.

"Makes sense, her being the youngest," John says.

Gawd.

Mitchell chuckles.

I hate being the baby.

Then his features smooth to serious. "Step back."

Everyone takes a cautious step backward exactly the way they came.

Mitchell plants his left foot behind his right as though he's at the starting line for a race.

Then he jumps.

I keep forgetting how strong zombies are until mine leaps from a nearly still position to a midair jump, sailing over the red grid line.

He twists before he lands with a single bouncing hop. Straightening, he moves quickly to where I stand. Mitchell's somber eyes meet mine. "Arms up, Deegan."

I nod but bite my lip. Terror makes my hands tingle. I lift my arms anyway.

Strong hands grip my wrists, and with a numbing jerk, I'm airborne.

I flip upside down and squeeze my eyes shut, thinking about my disheveled braid at the last second. *Is it long enough to hit the grid?*

I'm caught in his arms rather than the ground's hard embrace. A soft kiss lands on my forehead, then I'm set on my feet.

My eyelids burst open, and I let out air I didn't even realize I was holding.

It takes ten minutes to get everyone over. Mitchell never tires, ceaselessly chucking people.

Pax helps, everyone getting handed off to him or landing on him.

I do wonder if Mitch does a few tosses a little hard at my brother.

When he throws John over, Pax lands on his butt, with Uncle John on top. "Watch it, dead head." Pax scowls at Mitchell.

I catch Mitchell's small smile. *Pretty evil.*

For the millionth time, I wish my brother and my zombie could get along.

With a weary sigh, Kim pushes away from the old brick wall when everyone assembles. At an all-metal door that's shadowed by the deep sandwiching of the buildings proximity, she flips the cover up on an ancient keypad thing with softly lit numbers.

"Been a long time since I've seen one of those," Gramps remarks.

I've never seen one.

Kim punches in a code so quickly, it's obvious she's done it a lot.

The door lock disengages, and we walk into the building.

The first sound I hear is the soft whir of air conditioning and the unmistakable noiselessness of humanity in slumber.

That's where I want to be. Just thinking about a bed makes me realize how exhausted I am. My relief about getting through the grid without a fleet of bots descending feels almost anticlimactic simply because I'm too tired to give a crap.

The low-wattage antique LED lights don't burden my second lids too badly, but I retract anyway. I turn to tell Mitchell to retract his, but he already has.

There are no elevators in the building. Actual stairs mount the sides of the center of the building for up-and-down traffic, and we trudge over to the bottom.

I eye up the fresh slice of hell the stairs represent at the moment and sigh deeply.

"I *so* don't need this," Tiff comments, eyeing the offending staircase. "Cyber tech but no elevators? No pulse?" She shakes her head.

"Spot technology," Uncle John murmurs. "The absence of some things seem almost purposeful."

They do. It's weird the way they have bots but paranormals are kept in "camps." And the bots perform all the rudimentary tasks. And there are curfews.

And mass graves of future humanity.

My mind whirls. The cyborg mainframe is employing a sort of extinction process—of people.

I want to say so, to explain my revelation to the group, but Mitchell and I are at the end of the procession, and everyone is already at the top flight of stairs. I'll have to remember to say something.

"What are you thinking, Deegan?" Mitchell gives me a critical gaze, and I know I'm leaking some of my thoughts onto him. AftD is so much more intimate than just corpse raising.

I'm thinking so many things. But my ideas are too deep for discussion right now. I need to get rid of my menstrual cleanser, change it out—get clean.

I need food.

Mitchell accepts my silence and takes my hand, tugging me up the stairs.

I stop on number six, my right foot planted on the seventh tread. I sway where I stand. I *blink*, and my second eyelid can't even descend. Fatigue cripples me.

I feel my body lifted in strong arms.

Then I'm in Mitchell's cradle hold. He carries me effortlessly to the top of the flight of stairs.

"Now that's my kind of transport," Sophie says in an envious voice.

My head rolls in her direction against Mitchell's muscular bicep, and I give her a weak smile.

"I have two bathrooms," Kim says as we stream into her apartment.

Thank God.

Mitchell sets me on my feet for the second time in a half hour directly before the bathroom, and all us girls cram in there.

It doesn't take long to assess how primitive everything is. However, the best feature to the bathroom is the super-old tankless water heater mounted high on the wall abutting the ceiling.

Unlimited hot water. Yay.

The walk-in shower is of new construction, looking like a prototype for the next generations of showers we have in my world.

Showers where you can bathe if you're a man, woman, animal, wheelchair bound, and if need be, more than one person. Unibathing.

All of us strip while Kim goes into her bedroom and finds new clothing.

Mom, Sophie, Tiff, and I stuff ourselves into the large shower, sharing shampoo and soap.

I wash twice.

The water going down the drain carries dirt, blood, and woodland debris.

Mom uses a wide-tooth comb in an attempt to extract all the forest crap out of my hair, and finally shakes her head in resignation. "I don't know, Deegan—you might have to live with a more organic look for a little while. And no way on a braid." She smiles.

I feel so much better, I could sing, but I'll miss the tidiness of my braided hair. "No biggie. I just don't want to be gross anymore."

Tiff stuffs a stick of bright-pink gum in her mouth. "I hear that. I had a case of crusty crotch to beat the band."

We stare at Tiff.

Her eyebrows arch in clear amusement. "What? You guys were all flower-petal clean? *Pfft*." Tiff steps out of the shower, grabbing a towel, and whips her wet hair upside down. She begins toweling off then wraps the towel on her head, twisting it into a loose turban-style knot at the crown of her head.

She moves behind the shower wall and sits on the commode, figuring out the cleanser. "I miss tampons," she says after a few minutes of rustling around.

"Those are gross," I comment, wrinkling my nose. At the sink, I use the single new toothbrush we all have to share. I remember the part about tampon history in the part of *Bodily Function Accessories* perfectly. Yuck just doesn't cover it—and the damage to the environment!

Toxic shock syndrome? Yeah, great product, douches. And don't get me even started on *those*.

We rinse out our cleansers and reinsert. Mine is easy to put in, but Mom, Tiff, and Sophie have a few choice words about theirs.

I grin. Must suck to be tech-challenged. All of us teen girls were taught very thoroughly on the menstrual cleansers. After all, any of us who had the potential to have babies needed to know the fundamentals inside and out.

A soft knock sounds at the door.

"Come in," Sophie says, hugging the towel tighter around herself.

Kim comes in, gives us a look, and smiles. "Feel better? You guys smell better."

Gee, no kidding? I nod, and there are low sounds of general assent around the room.

She flops a big pile of clothes on a chair in the corner. "You'll have to mill through this stuff." I can tell Kim wants to say something more.

I search her face for a moment. "What?" I ask quietly.

"This was mine and my brother's place." She looks down for a second then lifts her chin, seeming to draw fortification from inside herself. "That's why I have a double apartment."

I had wondered. The space seemed big.

She blinks her eyelids rapidly, and I think she's keeping tears at bay. Kim inhales deeply. "Anyways, some of his things are in that pile, and some are mine. Use whatever fits best. The rest of his larger sized stuff is in the other bathroom for the guys."

Her swallow is so hard I hear it.

I walk over to her and pat her on the back. She's short, like me, and I decide she has the prettiest eyes I've ever seen. The only compassionate pair on bot world so far.

"I'm sorry that your brother's dead," I say softly.

Kim shakes her head fast. "Not dead."

Mom's and Sophie's heads simultaneously jerk in her direction, hands half-buried in the new pile of clothes.

"Then what?" Tiff asks. Not to be mean, but to be clear. It's just her way.

Kim wrings her hands, looking everywhere but at us. "He has been made Compliant."

My heart ticks faster, my mouth going dry. What the hell does *compliant* actually mean?

I ask that. None of us thought to question it before. What did we care? I mean—we're not from here. We're *blinking* back home soon.

So what if this world is messed up?

I gulp back my grief over the memory of the little ones' bodies, decomposed to just so much bone and rot. *Unraisable.*

My hand thumps in time with my accelerated heartbeats where the bone pierced the pad. Pax healed the wound, but it's not forgotten.

Bot world is desperately wrong, but it's not *our* faults. We have our own world to deal with.

"Compliant means when you cross over."

"Cross over?" Mom asks, the beginnings of horror edging her words.

Mom's meaning is clear to me. A thousand pieces of an elusive puzzle come together, and I lose my appetite completely.

Kim doesn't even have to explain. I already know what she's going to say.

"He's a cyborg now."

"Compliance isn't really *compliance* in the classical sense," Sophie says in a hushed voice of perfect understanding. "It's body-snatching."

Kim nods sadly. "Yes. That's why it was so important to avoid grid detection."

I shiver.

It would've been bad if we'd tripped their trigger.

19

Paxton

I place my hand on Dee's neck and give a soft squeeze. My poor sis, she's just not cut out for the stupidness that has become our lives.

First, we escape that Reflective world. Then I toss us back at bot world, where we get fucking lucky—there's no other way to look at that—and meet up with the single decent person in all of bot world.

But now I'm stuck with hangers-on. I have to get Kim *and* Ron the Null out of here.

I'm lucky that Tiff hasn't grilled me about where Bry landed yet, though I can feel he's on our homeworld somewhere, along with Archer. Probably too much for Tiff to own mentally now.

I shift my gaze to my healing handiwork on the Null dude's beak and see that it's still kind of crooked.

Dammit.

Gramps did a number on him. But seriously? Ron said something about Gramps thinking with his dick and wham.

I chuckle.

Gramps is pretty much a reactor. Like a nuclear reactor.

Not that we have that toxic shit for energy anymore. Talk about poisoning the planet. Now that's something for the enviro-emos to get fired up about. They did, and now we use our nearly endless natural gas supply, instead of burning it off to get at fossil fuel.

Dumb-ass concept.

Dee gives me a grateful look, and I pat her neck and drop my hand. We're totally different, but our bond goes beyond the sibling one—we *blink*. We raise corpses.

I snicker behind my hand. *Or convicts, in Dee's case.*

She punches my arm. Feels like a gnat bite. "Don't you dare laugh at me, Paxton."

She got a lot of my thought process through the old telepathy pipeline. I look directly into her scowl. "I'm laughing *with* you. Just thinking about all the prisoners you could raise here."

She shrugs, and I notice some crap in her hair. *Leaves? Huh.* But she smells a helluva lot better. 'Course—*so do I.* The only one who didn't have a shit ton of BO was Mitch. Zombies rot. And if they're not rotting, they don't smell like anything.

Clyde couldn't shower. Things would come off and clog the drain. Instead, he lounges in the corner, fingers laced and placed behind his head, feet crossed at the ankle as he surveys our group. He's relaxed, like our asses aren't plugged into a cyberworld channeling bots above humans.

"Okay humor aside, how ya feeling?" I ask Dee. Because the fact that her sucky cycle thought it was a good plan to make an appearance in the Kill World.

"Cramps."

"Oh."

Her dark-green eyes flash at me. "You asked."

"Yeah."

Kim grabs what looks like everything from her cupboards and puts a ton of food on a banquet-sized table.

I imagine her brother and whoever they hung with eating there. I think of Dee telling me about her brother not needing food anymore because he's a cyborg.

I shudder. Creeper bots.

"My turn," Kim says before making her way to the bathroom the women used.

She enters the bathroom and shuts the door to take her own shower.

"Let's talk about her behind her back," Tiff announces, glancing at the closed door.

"That's not very nice," Ron comments, working over the brim of his ten gallon in a nervous-tick kind of way.

"Go ahead," Dad says, drawing Mom in against his side.

Tiff flips Ron off. "Sit and spin, pal. You're here by our sufferance alone."

Gramps puts up his palm, and Tiff high-fives it.

"Fuck it," Jonesy says. "You guys discuss whatever deep subject matter you have in mind while I mow through the food."

Sophie groans, but Jonesy ignores her, tearing open five bags of chips and a bunch of chocolate-and-white sandwich wafer things called *Oreoes*.

Weird name.

"These look interesting." Jonesy sniffs then takes a tentative bite. "Love it." He gives a little moan, scooping up five more. "Different. Fatty." He waggles his brows.

Sophie gets interested and grabs one.

We listen to the shower turn on behind the closed bathroom door.

"Where's the moo?" Jonesy asks, and a black crumb falls off his lip and onto the table. He frowns, then his face brightens. "And beer for later?"

Disgusting. Beer and milk mentioned. Together.

"She doesn't have beer, ass," Tiff says.

"No Tiff, is the PMS a thing for ya right now?"

Tiff rolls her eyes. "That's *before* your cycle, Jones. I'm on it now."

Jonesy scrunches his eyes and puckers his lips. "I need more fuel to undo the snarl of your words. Besides, the Jonester doesn't pay much attention to the cycle part. It's the non-cycle part that's interesting."

The girls all appear to die, except Tiff.

"Right," Tiff replies in a droll word.

Jonesy sucks down a few more of the Oreos and begins to suck the crumbs off each finger.

I walk over to the fridge and scope a half gallon of milk. Personally, I find the drinking of cow's milk a reason to spew chunks.

But I walk over to the table and plop the glass jug down for Jonesy.

Uncle John frowns, turning the jar over in his palm and looking for the recycling logo.

"Everything's glass in the fridge," I comment in explanation, having noticed the lack of other storage material.

His eyes sharpen. "Perhaps plastics have been foregone in favor of the completely biodegradable glass."

Or they all go to the construction of bot-anity.

"That concept is more logical. In my day, there was no plastic. Food was always stored in glass. Tasted better, too." Clyde looks around the room as though waiting for a challenge.

A small chunk of scalp flops over as he moves his head, and a tuft of hair hangs distractingly upside down like a half open can lid.

Sophie gives the piece of dangling flesh a glance then turns away, looking a little green.

No dissenters voice their bullshit because we're all too busy shoving food in our mouths by the handful. I go back to the fridge and grab all the food that's left.

Deli meat, cheese, and a jar of pickles land on the table, along with a carbonated drink called Mountain Dew Throwback.

First ingredient: sugar.

"Oh, this is so bad for you kids," Mom says in despair. She twists a metal corrugated cap on one of them and takes a sip from the rolled-glass top. "Divine."

"Ali would be having convulsions right now." Gramps says with restrained glee, tossing back half a bottle. A loud belch erupts from his mouth half a second later. "Excuse me, folks."

Gramps doesn't seem very concerned by manners.

"Like an 'excuse me' even works like that half-barf burp you just sounded off. *Pfft.*" Tiff carefully sets her gum on the edge of a napkin and digs into the barbecue chips. "So about Kim?" she says, eyes on Gramps.

His narrow on her like smoky sapphires. "What about her?"

"She's Brad's second cousin once removed or something. *And* we've picked up Ron here."

I look at Ron. He's a lanky, lean hard-looking dude who's pretty beat up.

"They'll kill me if I stay now. Or"—he shivers— "make me Compliant."

"Yeah," I say, "let's discuss Compliance." I look to Dee. After a heartbeat's pause, she talks.

When the shower turns off and only crumbs remain where the food was, silence permeates the room.

Finally, Clyde says, "This world is even more danger-ous than ours."

That's a no-shitter. What was I thinking when I *blinked* us here? Oh yeah, I was getting us out of the last tight spot with those fuckers who were trying to recruit me. Nah, that was the first time. The last time was get-ting Dee away from the Brad of this world. I just keep coming back here. Gonna have to find a new parallel. This one blows.

And I'm not interested in being the new Graysheets version of AftD puppeteer. No thanks, dickbags.

"I believe, having seen the infanticide"—John glances at Tiff but her head is bowed, hands clasped, as though she refuses to acknowledge the awful mass grave—"that they are splicing and dicing humans with cyborgs. In a hundred years, this planet won't be a planet of humanity, but one of cyborg-human hybrids."

"How could things get like that. How is it *we* notice and the humans who live here are complacent?"

"One." Gramps holds up a finger. "We've got a fresh set of peepers on this business." He scans our faces. "Two, people here don't seem to be on fire to have kids. And why would they? The bots do all the dirty work. People can take it easy, not work for anything, and just get by with their credits and fill in wherever the bots don't need to be. And Thompson Enterprises has the zombies by the balls—"

"Or vagina," Tiff interjects neutrally, and I about spit out my pop.

Gramps smirks. "Right. Anyway, they need those AftDs to keep the zombie trade going, but the other humans? No."

"But it's like vampires," Dee says suddenly, and I have to remind myself she's a numbered IQ because, damn, this switch in topic makes no sense.

John nods.

"If there were vampires," she begins.

"That's horseshit," Jonesy says, stuffing the thirteenth Oreo into his mouth.

"Jones, quiet," Dad says, flipping his palm toward Dee.

Mitch shoots a dirty look at Jonesy like a speeding bullet.

"Anyway"—a small frown forms between her eyes—"say there's ten percent vampires in a world, and they can only live on human blood."

We wait, and she goes on. "If they just feed indiscriminately on *all* humans, pretty soon their diet is depleted and they die because there's no more food."

Vampires. What bullshit. I give an uneasy look-around, thinking about how bots seemed pretty out there, too. Until they were in our faces.

"Essentially," John says, clearly picking up on her thought process, "humans are still needed in some number for certain things."

"Like the zombie whoring," Sophie says in disgust.

I snort. "Yeah, I'd like to see a bot raise a dead guy."

"I'm not sure any of this matters," Mom says. "Pax will *blink* us home soon, and then we don't have to deal with the bot world."

Oh sure. So easy. Ask Archer and Bry how that went. They're probably getting their asses paddled by the handless sanction cops.

That makes a laugh pop out of my mouth like an untimely burp.

Dee gives me a strange look.

I can't keep it together. Funny visuals, Dee.

Nothing is funny about this, Pax. You and Dad always laugh when everything is serious. Stop being stupid.

I roll my eyes, and she folds her arms, glaring at me.

"Sounds simple," Tiff says. "Except I want to get knocked up."

We turn to Tiff, giving her open-mouthed surprise. Sometimes Aunt Tiff says shit that sucks the oxygen out of the universe.

John groans, hanging his head. "I know, honey. I know how badly you want a baby. But we can't stay in this dangerous place and risk our lives for the potential of a child. The *potential.*"

Tiff stands and strides over to her much-larger husband.

He looms over her, and Tiff obviously doesn't have any shits to give, poking him straight in the chest with her stiff pointer finger. "Listen, Terran"—poke—"I come from a very fertile family, and if this stupid"—poke—"Zondorae bullshittery hadn't happened, I'd be the happy mother of about a thousand little Johns or Tiffs."

John grabs her finger, kissing the tip. "Yes, very likely, but there are too many variables for us to risk it." His eyes are steady on her face. "To risk you. I can never risk you, Tiffany."

She tears her finger out of his grasp and folds her arms. John sits in the chair behind him and pats his lap. Tiff squints at him for a few seconds then huffs over there and sits down. John kisses the back of her neck, and she leans back against him. But her face is restless, unconvinced.

Disaster averted. For now.

"Tiff," Mom says, "what if we just get back home and try to get pregnant when we're ovulating in our world."

My head snaps to Mom. What if the baby's got webbed fingers? I mean—she's almost forty-two. Sort of ancient. Don't care if chicks are shooting out eggs like machine-gun fire in their forties, doesn't mean you should breed.

"What if it doesn't work?" Sophie asks softly.

All the men sigh. *Women want babies.*

I smirk. We guys sure want to give them to women. I mean, is there a guy alive that doesn't want to spread his seed? Crude, but true. Hard to separate that from that protect-the-chick instinct, too. It's all mixed up together.

It's a dilemma. But we can't make babies if we're *dead*. And the longer we hang in bot world, the more chances we have to get dead.

Or Compliant, which sounds way worse.

Before we can discuss her in detail, Kim comes out, her hair wrapped in a cream towel and piled on her head.

Gramps jerks his thumb at her. "She's coming, end of discussion."

I guess that's that.

"What?" she asks. Her large eyes seem even bigger without the distraction of her dark hair everywhere.

"We don't know if we want to bring a Thompson relative to our world," Tiff says bluntly, still clearly pissed at John.

"I see," she says, her gaze taking in the remnants of the food. Her eyes well with tears. After all, we've totally encroached on her space, and Brad the Chump should be coming along any moment to fuck things seven ways to Sunday, as Dad likes to say.

Gramps doesn't miss anything about her altered state. "You're *blinking* with us."

She nods, eyelids fluttering back the tears as she wallops in breath that depletes the oxygen in the room.

I don't know if her tears are grateful or sad. Can't tell that shit. With Dee, I can see if she's sad. With my mind.

Do you want Kim to come? I send to Dee.

Yeah, she's good, Pax.

I thought so, too. Having Dee echo my thinking makes it legit.

Sophie stands suddenly. A stricken expression tightens her features like a corkscrew. Her bluish-green eyes are slits. "I can't find my purple purse."

Wow, let's alert the media. My eyes find the big orange monstrosity on one of the chairs. I point to that. "Isn't that—"

"Nope," Jonesy interrupts, having moved on to licking Cheeto dust from his fingers. *Hog.* "That's the big purse. There's a little one that looked like those hot pants Jade was wearing."

Oh yeah, a vague memory of a glittery purple thing with puffy lips surfaces in the front of my brain. "Okay…" I jerk my shoulders to my ears.

Her lips thin with anger.

My bad.

"It was attached to my orange handbag."

Still not getting the importance.

Uncle John jumps up from the chair, nearly upending Tiff from his lap. "The grid."

Kim's eyes widen. "Could it have become lost when we were tossed into my alley?"

The room goes silent.

"Do you remember having your handbag when Mitchell threw you over the grid end?" John asks tersely.

Sophie gives a miserable nod.

"What's happening?" Mom asks.

"What's happening is Sophie dropped her mini-purse on the grid."

"It's been triggered?" Kim asks in a voice squeezed down to a wheezing whisper.

"Hold on, guys," Gramps says, hand absently patting his pocket.

Kim walks over to a drawer and pulls something out. "These were my brother's."

"Contraband?" Gramps asks, with a twinkle in his eye, as he grabs the pack of cigarettes.

She grins, but the smile is a tense grimace. "Absolutely."

"I do think a lot better with some nicotine."

"Amen," Clyde says, coming to life in the corner.

Gramps lights up, shoots out a smoke ring the size of my neck, and says, "Looks like we better blow this Popsicle stand before the bots come and try to rearrange our body parts, I suppose."

"Am I still coming?" Ron asks.

His voice does come out clearer now that I re-broke and healed his nose after our supper of deli meat, chips, and those cookie things.

Gramps whips his palm around, filling the space with the sick smoke. "We don't know for sure that Sophie's purse fell on the grid. It could have just as easily fell on the alley side."

We stare at him for a few seconds.

Then an earsplitting wail of sirens pierce the air.

"Or not!" Gramps says, standing.

Kim pivots, runs to the door, and engages the dead-bolt. Her hands tremble. She puts her palms flat against the door. "I can't be Compliant."

Gramps walks to her, putting the stub of his lit cigarette out on the deep tread of his boot. He puts the butt behind his ear and leans over the back of her body.

"There aren't enough thugs to get you from us, Kim. Stay close, and we'll see who's Compliant."

She turns in his arms and puts her face against his chest. "I'm scared," she whispers.

"It's all right, sweetheart. I've never been one to comply anyway," Gramps comments.

No shit.

Then something thuds against the door, rattling the frame. And Gramps pulls her behind him.

"They're here," Kim says mournfully, fisting the flannel shirt Gramps wears.

"Fuck," Tiff spits in what sounds like a resigned bark.

"Yeah," I agree.

"Bring it," Mitch says, and I frown at him.

Never heard that one before. "Bring what?" I ask through the blaring.

His sharp blue eyes are ice chips in a hard face. "Whatever they can. They will not have my mistress."

He's halfway to Dee when the door cracks through the middle, a metal battering ram impaling its center like a toothpick through a tongue.

In walks Brad. Well, in *limps* Brad. And some guy who has Kim's eyes, but the body of a bot.

20

Brad

There's the miserable little cunt.

Right there. Looking a tiny bit worse for wear.

I squint. *Are those leaves in her hair?*

Whatever.

Deegan Hart is in sight. I wouldn't admit it in our world, but I wanted to nail her. Bad. This not-being-able-to-produce-kid's thing has made every guy on earth rabid. But they want to protect the bitches, too. I don't have that problem, thankfully. See, when hardly anyone can even have kids, women somehow are worth more. Yeah. *Right.* They're worth the value I assign them. And Deegan has always rubbed me the wrong way. I thought she would be impressed with my wealth and obvious good looks on our home earth.

She wasn't.

The more I pushed and tried to win her over with that fake, syrupy romance shit most bitches dig, the more she avoided me. Then I started just hassling her—stealing her energy and whatnot.

I would love to just cement her negative reaction to my advances in the fact that she's just too *dumb* to know a good thing when she sees it.

But that wasn't it. No. She's numbered. Deegan Hart is smart enough to know I wanted to sample the wares and take whatever I felt like. Practically a Thompson legacy. Not giving. I wasn't going to offer her anything but a fun time. And maybe another go if I liked sticking it to her.

But Deegan's too smart for that. Somehow, she knows my intentions. And that fucking Body, corpse-humping, psycho parallel world shifter brother of hers is *always* lurking around like an overprotective shadow.

Hate his ass.

No longer. The cyborgs here covertly terminate all children by mandate, in stark contrast to my earth, where conversations stops at the sound of a child's voice. The cyborg world leaves only a small percentage who have the potential for something worthwhile. Translation: Paranormal abilities to manipulate in some way.

I salivate looking at Deegan. She's got the DNA I need to pump my way into this world before the cyborgs completely take over. Before they start wailing about AftD, Empath and the rest, if I can get a few of those parallel-shifting spawn out of her, the worlds I can control would be limitless.

I signal to my other cousin, now a quite-willing cyborg, and he knocks the head off the nearest cyborg that won't quit its caterwauling. These fucking cyborgs are even more persistent than zombies. And that's saying something. I know, having been on the receiving end of zombie diligence.

Deegan is not the only numbered IQ in the room. Mine is nearly one-seventy. I'm top dog on this other blue marble. Smart enough to fuck everyone up. This world is much better for who I am. Too bad I can't just move back and forth between my home earth and this one. I need a Pax for that. Can't control him, though.

It'd be fun to try.

That's why Daddy Dearest lets me run the sleazy zombie show. Once the AftDs take the spunk out of the female zombies and make them alive, they're quite fun to force into whatever little game I feel like playing.

The horror of them *knowing* they must obey is too special to ignore. Fear standing in their eyes is like a drug. It's my new addiction. Of course, a few AftDs have been unwilling to force the zombies they raise to do what needs doing.

We eliminate those dissenters. It's a loss, though. AftD is a rare ability. And raising corpses requires at least a level four on this earth. Interesting how the phrasing and terminology is just a hair off my home world's verbiage.

After I conquer Deegan and get a new strain of paranormals—only the powerful type, of course—then I can branch out in other areas.

Other worlds.

I don't have my ability-stealer talent on this world either. Otherwise, I could just rob Deegan of her abilities and her energy then just keep her around for basic recreational use. Like a nifty fuck toy.

My grin fades as I remember I'm basically a mid-level AftD in cyborg-and-zombie paradise. That makes my use of the zombies all the sweeter.

My talents here are insufficient for autonomous recreational entertainment.

What we could do with some *blinkers* in the family, as the Hart clan refers to Pax's ability…

"Deegan." I glance down at the decapitated cyborg and breathe out a sigh of mixed disgust and relief at the sudden silence. Dad will be pissed at the loss of that. Each cyborg is critical for Compliance assurance. My eyes narrow at the slip of a girl I've been chasing all over the place.

Her face isn't anything special. She's not classically pretty. High cheekbones and coal-black hair frame eyes that are deep green, like the forest. Deegan is exotic, not pretty. Still, her lack of perfection doesn't make her less desirable. I want her more. She has a face people remember after only seeing once.

That face currently glares defiantly at me. I will love *breaking* that spirit.

I take in the mofo at her right. Now that's a big damn zombie. He's indigenous to the planet. At least, that's what the cyborgs tell me.

I don't like the way he hovers around her. But she raised him, so them there is the breaks.

"Let me introduce myself properly—now that the noise has died down."

I bestow my benevolent smile on their little posse.

Deegan's great-grandpa stares back with a look that should incinerate me into a pile of ashes.

He'll be the first one we make Compliant. Mac O'Brien was a pain in the ass in my world. And now that I've been helpfully *blinked* to this world, I have the means to see my agenda through. And I so fucking will.

"Miscreant."

I look toward the voice that uttered that one word.

A rotting pile of slop looks back.

I frown. Don't like the bright eyes of that zombie. Looks like he's about ready to pull something out of his degrading bag of tricks. I remember he's one of the first to be raised in our world. What was his name?

I tap my chin. *Claude?*

Whatever. He gets second slot after old grandpa, who's obviously had regeneration.

Can't make the dead Compliant. But there's always the blow torch. I scrunch my nose. This world has some primitive bullshit I don't like at all. Then again, it has some stuff that's mighty fine. Like the zombie whore houses that I run.

My attention turns back to Deegan. Now, if she had just let the Brad of this world have his way with her, I wouldn't be in this little disaster.

There would be two Brads to one Deegan.

Speaking of which. I signal Harry, my right-hand cyborg cousin, a second time, to call in the sneaky Ace in my deck of cards.

A moment later, Jeffrey Parker strolls through.

The looks on their faces! Best. Thing. Ever.

Gramps

Parker strolls in.

Fuck a duck.

"Hi, guys." He smiles. Mr. Congeniality.

He hops over the downed bot, halts in front of our loose group, and nods absently. His surreal presence is not to be outdone.

The other Parker comes in directly after him.

Beaten.

Tied.

Gagged.

That's our boy. Getting the Bot Hospitality first-class treatment.

Jeffrey Parker is older now than when we first made acquaintance with each other. I suppress a chuckle—probably about my regeneration age that I am now.

Our Jeffrey's sharp gaze finds me. He blinks, and those hard hazel eyes tell me a lot.

He's been tortured. The Parker I know would never deign to raise corpses for their little pimp-and-whore byplay. Nope.

So he's paying the price for his resistance. Looks like he has more broken than unbroken fingers, and I can more or less see one whole eyeball. The other is hidden by swollen and reddened flesh.

But they've got their Parker, who appears to have a flock of geese banging away in that skull of his. Fruitcake.

Bet he's numbered, like our Deedie. That would mean he's insane *and* brilliant. Not a good combo.

I tap my breast pocket, and a few smokes flop around in there. Suppose I should be freaking out about our future about now. But I've never been one to panic.

Figure something will present itself for me to use. Not sure what, at present. Things are looking a tad grim.

"Please, Brad—think about what you're doing. What you're committing to." Kim's eyes move between Brad and the bot I assume used to be her brother.

Brother Bot stares back impassively.

Bad.

Thompson hikes an eyebrow, jerking his square pretty-boy jaw back, and barks a chuckle. "Listen, cousin,

I don't care if you're a relative or even if you can still birth a child."

Hmm. News to me. I study Kim in a new light.

"You clearly kept some amazing Healer skills under wraps while springing these other-world birds from jail. We had special spots in the camps just for them." Brad's eyes sweep everyone.

Camps. Ah yes. The paranormal Auschwitz of bot world.

"Brad," Kim pleads, shooting a furtive glance toward the bot whose eyes resemble hers. Though his are on the cold side. Like frozen molasses.

No help on that front.

Brad tosses a casual punch to Jeff's solar plexus.

I tense as Jeff grunts, eyes watering.

"You lowlife," Caleb growls.

Yup. I'd love to give this punk an esophagus love tap. I eyeball his Adam's apple with pure lust.

Thompson whips up a palm. "Parker's been fun to work over. Stubborn as the day is long."

Jeff's eyes plead with mine. He seems to be trying to tell me something.

I remember my strange little teleporting number I pulled in the Rome world—or Papilio—*blinking* soldiers.

Wonder if I'll get lucky here?

I concentrate, trying to scoop into that well that seemed to be full when I was in that other strange world.

Nothing.

I feel each beat of my regenerating heart. I read the fine print on the pulseforms, about how the potential side effects were a longer list than the bennies. Didn't matter. What mattered was eking out a little more time in this life to annoy my family.

I grin at the thought of still kicking around at one hundred—or better yet, the new life expectancy marker that's been predicted to top out at around one hundred thirty-five.

"What are you smiling about, Mackenzie?" Brad asks, tone seething. "You have nothing to be happy about. You and your useless band of familial rodents will be thrown into the camps for use as our wonderful cyborg-run government sees fit. And a few scientists have an interest in some of the abilities manifesting in your family." His smile grows broader. "An avid interest."

Ignoring his prattling on, I rifle through my head, trying to find what Jeff seems so intent to communicate with me.

There. Shock bites at me. *No. That can't be right.*

The fine print had said in rare instances, dormant genetic markers would manifest as the body frog-leaped backward in its biological clock. Almost like a puberty do-over.

I ignored that tiny fine print. Who would ever, for any reason, want to return to adolescence? Miserable time of life.

Yet, here I am, having gone through the regeneration without a bleep of any side effects on the radar.

In my home world.

But *here*? Here is another matter entirely. Apparently, my regeneration process is still active. I'm nine months deep in the year-long journey of the biological clock of my body ticking backward. The entire method mimics a second adolescence.

I whip my head to look at Jeffrey. His exhale of relief is muffled through the gag.

He nods.

Fear never rules me. It never has. But now, terror makes my lips grow numb. My fingertips tingle with the familiar beginnings of adrenaline so powerful that bile rises in my stomach.

"Gramps?" Jade says in a voice of pure panic.

Must be getting some leakage. I know anyone who is remotely sensitive would be tuning up for what I was about to do.

My last glance is at Deedie.

Sorry, Deedie. Gramps is getting his groove on.

Then I go Atomic. Not like my great-granddaughter. A new thing.

21

Deegan

Everyone discounts the old.

Not me.

I watch the entire sequence of looks that pass between our Jeffrey Parker and Gramps.

I see when Gramps seems to understand Jeff's silent message.

I feel Gramps when he finds his ability. It is so much like when Pax uses AftD around me that I know instantly when Gramps is using black-hole mojo.

He sweeps past me. A blur of denim and finely checkered old-guy button-down shirt whirls beside me, lifting the fine tendrils of hair beside my temples. His pack of cigarettes floats out of his front pocket as he surges by, and I reach up into his tailwind, grabbing them out of air so stagnate, it feels stale.

The remaining bots are beginning to open their mouths. I'm pretty sure they don't know what it is Gramps *has*. They just know it's a Bad Paranormal Skill.

I slap my hands over my ears.

Whatever he's doing, it's a form of Atomic.

But what *is* he doing? *I don't know.*

Pax's head turns in my direction. It takes him ten seconds to turn.

Our eyes lock.

Dee, blink.

Yes, comes my slowed telepathic reply.

We *blink* at the same time.

What did the Reflectives call it? Oh, yeah—a primary ability. An ability that remains no matter where you *blink* to. That's their theory, anyway.

Second eyelids sweep over our eyeballs. And I sigh. Suddenly, Pax and I can move at normal speed.

Gramps turns, zipping his ceramic blade through Jeff's binds. He begins to float to the ground.

Pax easily catches him before he lands.

Jeff raises his eyes. "Keep hold of me, and I can move at normal speed."

"How'd you know, Jeff?" Pax asks in wonder.

"Later. For now, just know I intuit everyones' abilities on this world. It's an ability in and of itself."

Oh.

Jeff's eyes find mine. He sucks in a painful inhale. "Zap the cyborgs, Deegan."

My palms develop fine sweat. My fingers tremble. And I voice my deepest uncertainty. "What if I get one of us by accident?"

Mitchell is suddenly there. He *blinked*, and now he can move like Pax and me. He grabs my hand, lacing our fingers.

In my periphery, I see Brad making slow gestures. Actually, he's trying to move toward me. He can borrow my abilities in our world.

What can he do here?

Jeff's hand swims toward mine, and I grasp it. I hold my zombie in one hand and my Dad's mentor in the other.

Ah. I see what he's trying to do.

He gasps. "I'll facilitate with your finesse. It's short range, but it'll get rid of this group."

Jeff is going to steer the paranormal helm, so to speak. That way, I don't take out everyone at the knees.

"No!"

Gramps's atomic mass manipulation swallows Kim's scream. Her yell is twenty seconds long and sounds like it's coming toward us like a train through a tunnel.

I look at Harry, her brother the bot. "She doesn't want me to make Harry—" *Go wherever I put things I zap.*

Mitchell draws me back against him, and my fingers stay laced with Jeff's.

Jeff's wounds are so severe, I can barely see his expression past the injuries.

I suck in a breath and tighten my hand on his. I feel his crushed finger and remember my own from this world.

A bot has made it all the way to a meter in front of me. I'm so scared, I taste metal in my mouth. "Mitchell."

"Right here, baby. Make these fuckers disappear, Deegan."

Hot tears cascade down my face. I nod, but it's hardly more than a jerk of my chin.

I release the power in a relieved sigh of exhaustion.

Jeff's body tenses, and he narrows my ability like a beam of light. In this case, it's a swath of darkness as though a knife slices pieces from the air. Carving space and time.

The first bot is eaten from where it stood.

Everything around it is there one moment, and in the next, the air sucks inside itself, making a popping sound. The spot on the floor where the bot stood has vanished, leaving a gaping hole instead, and I get a glimpse of the apartment below.

The group behind that initial bot is easier.

They're yawning mouths are first to go. Disappearing like black measles appearing in the middle of their silver, slightly glowing, and opaque faces. The silence is big where their horrible mechanical screaming was before.

Gramps collapses beside me, his hand grabbing my knee. "Tired," he manages.

Yeah, welcome to the club. Rearranging mass at the atomic level takes a lot out of someone.

He sped himself up, and Pax and I *blinked* so we could move within the altered environment he'd made.

Brad lies on the floor, knocked out cold by Gramps. A swelling eggplant-colored bruise competes with his Adam's apple.

But the other Jeff's been busy.

Zombies, in various states of decomposition, fill the doorway. But they're bright like the now-defunct copper pennies. Ready.

The false Parker smiles. He can't move fast, but he's called reinforcements.

I cast one more net of zapping juice, winking out the last of the bots within the apartment, because they're the biggest threat.

Except Kim's brother.

Then Gramps's ability fizzles away, righting the mass of the room back to normal.

Before I can get the enemy zombies.

Mitchell's grip intensifies as I experience vertigo that I would have collapsed from. But Mitchell is here.

Holding me.

"Impressive, Mac. But not enough." The fake Parker nods, and the zombies press through the doorway, stumbling over Brad's still form.

"Not on my watch, Parker," the real Jeff says from the ground.

"Outta juice, Deedie," Gramps says at my feet.

I pry myself away from Mitchell, searching for Pax, Gramps's hand at my calf.

Pax has Mom and Dad. "Pax," I yell, "*blink* us!"

The zombies come. Hungry. Their appetite beats at me with small clubs, making my head ache.

They know Pax and I are AftD—Tiff too.

They just don't care.

The Parker of this world is a five-point squared.

Gramps provided a distraction. But that's all. That's the way it goes with a new ability. It was great that he could even use it with any kind of finesse.

I pivot slowly, taking in the group. "If anyone has anything, now is the time to use it." *Please*, I pray.

My ability has made me sick. I'm scooped out. A muscle I've been effectively trained out of using.

Sophie comes forward. "It might not be enough."

It.

"Doesn't matter," I say as Mitchell jerks me away from the nearest zombie's outstretched fingers.

Use whatever it is, I silently bellow at Sophie.

She jerks like she heard me.

The grasp of the fingertips of the nearest corpse slides through my hair, latching on.

The tug is hard, and I get yanked backward.

Mitchell grips the zombie's arm, twisting the limb viciously.

The zombie clutches my hair tighter. I instinctively shriek from the pain.

"Deegan!" Sophie yells.

"Do it!" I scream back.

I feel the shift of her power from deep inside, and my stomach bucks from yet another physical scramble.

The apartment melts away.

Mist covers us, and we're like tea leaves steeping in foggy water. Then we land—all of us.

Right on top of the grid.

The sun rises as Pax and I automatically retract our eyelids.

Oh… no.

Mitchell tries to keep his open, but they won't stay in the descended position. It's just like looking at the sun. A person *can*, but self-preservation eventually kicks in. Just like you can stop from blinking several times a minute—but we can't keep our second eyelids down when natural sunlight makes an appearance.

The bots will come, but the zombies aren't close anymore.

I take a shaky breath.

"Sweet, baby," Jonesy says to Sophie, clearly impressed.

She bursts into tears. "All you fat asses! That's as far as I could teleport you."

I laugh and can't stop until I cry.

22

Gramps

Right out of the frying pan and right into the fire. *I need a vacation.* From my life.

Since I'm not pals with the boss of this little journey, I figure I've got to show up and do my job. Sort of a work-without-pay program. Didn't sign up for that.

Since I'm not one for crying in my Wheaties, I'll keep on keeping on.

For the third time in days, I'm parked on my old ass. I do a quick ground search for Kim (keeping tabs on Kim seems to be my new priority), and a speedy head count.

We got everybody. A miracle.

Sophie even managed the body dump with Jeff tagging along.

"Pax," I say, hiking my butt off the ground with a palm-to-knee shove-off. I pat the grass and debris off my keister.

Grandkid turns to me, looking better. Funny what about three thousand calories will do for the twenty-year-old male of the species. And a Body to boot. All sugar and carbs. Snack of champions.

"Yeah, Gramps."

"Fix Jeff up—looking a bit shaky." *Maybe that's an understatement.*

Jeff is gulping air through his ruined nose like a swimmer doing a shitty version of the crawl stroke in a swimming pool. Looks like most of his fingers are definitely broken.

They sure have a thing for breaking fingers in the bot world.

Pax winces, jogging to Jeff. "How did you even— wow, how did you help Deegan with the mess you're in?" Even as he asks the question, Pax covers Jeff's nose. The glaring injury is among the worst ones.

Looks like he's suffocating him without the benefit of a pillow.

Jeff's eyes widen, but Pax presses down harder.

Jeff grabs his wrists, tears sliding out his eyes. That guy isn't sad. He's tougher than nails.

The tears are simply an off pouring of agony.

Slowly, Pax begins to lift his hand millimeter by millimeter, and Parker's nose appears to regrow, shaping back into an appendage to assist airflow instead of a discarded flapjack of blood and cartilage.

"Thanks," Jeff says without gurgling, dropping his hands to his sides in an exhausted flop.

Pax's large hand hovers over Jeff's neck. "Bruised esophagus," Pax comments in a mild, dreamy voice. His long fingers wrap Jeffrey's throat.

Ten seconds slide by—then twenty.

Jeff coughs, grimaces from obvious pain, and sits up, using his damaged hands. He shouts in agony, clutching one broken set of fingers with the other.

In my periphery, Deegan covers her mouth. I'm certain she's remembering her little go with the Brad Thompson of this world before we were able to get to her. And end him.

She told me her fingers still ache when it rains. There's just some ways fingers aren't meant to be bent.

I hate these guys here.

"Hey, give me a sec, Jeff."

Jeffrey Parker's bright-hazel eyeball blinks slowly, and he jerks his head in a miserable nod of assent, eyes shiny.

Pax presses a finger to his distended eyeball. The slit widens. The swelling recedes like a wave pulling away from a red shore. Pax lifts his finger and gives a hard look to his dad, John, and Jonesy. They walk over, each one using their body weight to pin down Jeff's limbs.

Shit's about to get real.

Our two zombies stand guard. One is a soup of rot, and the other is like a fresh daisy. The women look on in stunned horror. Except Tiff. She's a hard-charging bitch on wheels.

Wouldn't have her any other way. She has my heart in her hands; she always has. I look at all the kids, technically grown now. Pieces of Mac reside in each one of these precious people. Once kids, they're now more adult than they ought to be.

Pax takes Jeffrey's dominant right hand in his own, and Jeff breathes through his mouth like he's in a Lamaze birthing class.

Pax re-breaks Jeff's pointer finger with a snapping sound that reminds me of things better not remembered.

Jeff passes out on number four.

His mouth hangs agape, and Pax continues with his grim work of breaking and mending.

Tears fill Kim's eyes. "God have mercy," she says on a hot breath.

Yes, that sounds about right.

"*Your* family did this," Caleb say, voice disgusted.

Ron the Null scoots back, attempting to avoid the verbal line of fire.

Have fun with that.

I shoot Caleb a glare. "Listen, son—I think we've established the fact that Kim is escaping this fun little place, eh? She's not diggin' the family dynamic much." I lift my eyebrows, hitting the breast pocket of my shirt with a tap of my fingertips and finding it empty.

Damn.

Deedie laughs, holding up crushed cigarettes in her palm.

But one remains whole and sound.

I stride over there—being in motion feels good. I pluck the cancer stick out of her hand, briefly mourning the others as so much pulverized tobacco.

Oh well.

I dig through the front pocket of my slacks and scoop out a pack of matches. The sulfur strip is screwed six ways to Sunday, so I use the tread of my boot to light up.

I puff away.

Sublime.

"Now what?" Ron asks, his eyes bouncing around everyone.

I squint through my smoke at him. "You're along for the ride, Null Master. The girls have vouched for ya, but I remain unconvinced."

"Jury is still out," Clyde remarks, but it comes out so sloppy, I'm pretty sure only people familiar with the turn of phrase could translate it. I look at our good zombie friend and relative. Better I don't get a good look. Even through the veil of my smoke, Clyde looks terrible.

"I'm not soft in my evaluations," Tiff says, eyeing Ron up.

I nod. That's true. Tiff Weller's a ball buster.

"And for the record, I think it blows you keep cropping up with smokes and I'm dryer than a popcorn fart." Tiff waggles her thumb and pinky toward her open mouth in a seesaw motion.

John slaps his forehead.

"Can't have you seven sheets to the wind, Tiff," I comment.

She snorts.

"Besides, you want to be this baby-maker. You can't drink while you're pregnant." I shrug.

"Yeah, get sauced after the baby's born," Jonesy recommends instantly.

I sigh.

"*That's* why I want to stay here and take my chances."

"Are you listening, Tiff?" Jonesy asks. "Look around. This baby-murdering, finger-breaking, Torture World with these creeper bots is a *no-go*. I don't care if Terran can inseminate you with octuplets. I wanna go home."

Tiff scowls stubbornly. "Then go, bird brain. Pax can *blink* back here and round up us chicks after we've done the deed."

"Don't you have one hundred and ten nieces and nephews?" Jonesy asks, flipping his palms up.

"Bite me, Jones."

Jonesy laughs, shaking his head.

Deegan groans, and I laugh, too. Can't help it. Tiff tickles me pink—when she's not drunk.

"Honey. Tiff…" John says, trying for reason.

I smirk when she throws up a warding hand. "The zombies are still milling around at Kim's place. Sophie dumped us into the grid, so we should be expecting Bot Reinforcements any second." She looks around for dissenters, and of course, there aren't any, because she's right as rain.

"Tiff, you know that as women of our world, we should be doing some kind of"—Jade's palm waffles back and forth—"obligatory 'duty' for humankind."

"Hell, yeah," Jonesy says, nodding enthusiastically.

I scrub a palm over my face, rasping my two days of stubble in an irritated swipe.

Sophie gives him the bird.

Jade glares at Jones and he grins, unrepentant.

"But we can't be mothers if we're all dead." Jade looks at the other girls.

I think of Ali and how much less my life would mean without her in it. And that wonderful daughter of mine gave me Caleb—and the kids who do these extraordinary things. My chest swells, tight with an emotion I'll never vent. The feeling sits there nonetheless, reminding me that my family is my greatest weakness—my greatest strength.

I would do anything for them.

Tiff sulks. "Can't Sophie just pop us into like—a hotel or something."

Hmmm. I give Kim what I hope is a covert glance.

She smiles back. *Nope. Not so covert.*

I dip my chin, trying to hide my grin at getting caught ruminating about sex.

Sophie pegs a hand at her hip. "I *totally* would if I think I could manage it, but there's so *many* of you." She blows a stray spiral curl out of her face, sees me looking, and self-consciously tucks the errant lock behind her ear. "No product here," she mutters as the piece of hair stubbornly springs back.

"The bots *will* come," Ron says.

What a wet blanket, I think, puffing away.

Jeffrey finally comes around to the land of the living and graces Pax with a sluggish smile.

Pax grins. "Good to have you back, Jeff."

He slaps his palm into Pax's.

Pax jerks him to a standing position. Jeff winces, flexing his newly healed digits. "Good to be back." He looks around. "Hell—if I've got our bearing correct, we're on top of the detection grid."

"Sorry," Sophie says, voice contrite.

He waves that away. "It's fine, had a bunch of brain-loving zombies up our ass." He looks at Mitchell and Clyde. "No offense."

Mitchell shrugs. "Clearly, this is a case of 'it is what it is.'"

Jeff looks to Caleb. "Get me up to speed, Hart."

I snuff my smoke out on the bottom of my boot and flick the butt. "*The Reader's Digest* version, Caleb."

"Right, Gramps." Caleb looks at Jeff. "Basically, Pax *blinked* us out of *our* earth then accidentally, we went to a world full of *blinkers*, but apparently they don't do *parallel* worlds. But actual, primary earths."

"They call them *sectors*—there's thirteen. And they tell us we're 'threes,'" John adds.

I nod, swirl my hand, notice my second cig is a dead butt, and snuff it out.

"Thirteen earths?" Jonesy asks, frowning.

"Yeah," Pax replies.

"All I know is I could raise the dead on that earth, and it sucked balls. Plus, their hospitality also blows. Big time." Jonesy spreads his hands. "I want to torch the bad guys, not be a corpse-monger."

Caleb, Tiff, and Pax shoot him a dirty look.

"Whatever!" Jonesy slaps his thighs, muttering something about beer and football.

"Anyway," Caleb says, gifting Jonesy a final, dark look, "we barely escaped the mess of that world, and Pax *blinked* us back here, right into Thompson's fun and games."

"Dad," Pax says reproachfully.

"Dad is not saying it's your fault," Jade comments.

Pax starts copping an attitude, and I sigh. "I *had* to get us out of our world, Mom." He crosses his arms, planting his legs wide, a deep furrow between his eyes.

Deedie looks at Pax. "Because of the undead you pulled from this world," she points out.

He scowls at her.

Damn kids.

Deedie lifts a shoulder. "Listen, you know I love you, Pax, but when George and his family suddenly showed up—unsanctioned dead—the cops were called."

Pax's eyes narrow on his sister. "And don't forget loverboy." He jerks his jaw toward Mitch. "He had to come back, too. They *definitely* noticed him."

Mitchell's bright eyes become slits of blue flame. "You know, I'm about sick of you. If it weren't for me, Deegan would be dead. She summoned me because she was against the wall, Hart. Not because I would be her lover. She's seventeen, for God's sake."

Deegan's exhale is disgusted.

"And like you care about *that*?" Pax asks in a low voice.

Mitch's face tightens down like a drum. "Fuck yes, I care. I'm her *zombie*. You know exactly how much I care, you spoiled, fat-headed asshole."

Deegan latches on to the back of Mitch's shirt. As though that would keep the big fella contained. She rests her forehead against his back, and he stills.

"Boys," I say in warning, wishing for another smoke and figuring I'll have to forgo that pleasure in lieu of attitude adjusting.

It always comes back to that.

"Can you *blink* us back to earth—our earth?" Jade asks Pax, trying like hell to ignore the testosterone bomb ready to explode.

Pax's eyes move from Mitch to his mom's. "I can." He sounds suspicious of her point.

I'm relieved by his reply. I'm ready to split. Regardless of the girls' mixed feelings of fertility, I share the opinion that they can't get pregnant if they're dead.

"Can you *blink* us inner-world?" Tiff asks suddenly.

Pax's exhale is a raw breath. "Not with perfect accuracy," he admits.

So it's all or nothing for Pax.

We look at Sophie. "I've used my ability one time."

Yeah, and here we stand on the grid.

Jeff drags a hand over his skull several times, finally saying, "Listen, the evil that we know and all that. My counterpart of this world is trying to use me to identify all paranormals." He faces Pax. "He wants someone who can *blink* from here. His very own Pax. If he finds that— he and Clement Thompson's brat can travel to all the parallels and corrupt those. He will. We need to get *me* the hell out of *here*. And you." He looks at each woman, his eyes landing last on Tiff. "Sorry, ladies—the safety of all these parallel worlds is up to us. We get me out of here and back to our home world. It's more important than fertility, babies—any of that." His eyes remain on Tiff.

She shifts her weight, shooting daggers with her eyes. "I'm not stupid, Parker."

"Oh... I'm aware." Jeff smirks.

"But you're blinded by the potential to have children that this world offers, Tiffany," John says.

I knot my hands in defeat, waiting this out.

"Yeah," she says, small fists at her sides. "I am. So let's get out of here before I can think about what I'm gonna lose by going."

"It's daytime. The grid is not activated during that time," Kim says into the weighted silence.

"Before I *blinked*, I saw it, though," Deedie says, sounding doubtful.

I can't see the grid. I'll take the kids' word for it. There's been entirely too many coincidences.

I've never been a big believer in those.

"We're going to encounter some unpredictable things when we return," Caleb says, then suddenly, his face lifts—eyes tight. "Onyx."

"He's okay," Deedie says. "I left his doggie door open."

Caleb's shoulders slump in clear relief. "Thank God. I don't think he'd welcome the Sanction cops into our humble abode."

Jade's shoulders begin to shake with her silent sobs. Can't say I blame her. I wouldn't want the SPs stomping through my home, either.

Caleb hugs her, and she buries her face in his chest.

Pax gives an abrupt chuckle. "No way he hung around the house. Onyx is long gone by now—in Scenic Cemetery."

The group breathes easier. Everyone loves that half-dead dog. He's Caleb's, but he's also the entire gang's, in a strange way.

Of course, he might be a little worse for wear now because Caleb is here, not there, helping Onyx stay "alive" with his AftD. He seems to perk up around cemeteries, though. I brighten. It's a small silver lining, but I'll take anything positive at the moment.

Tiff kicks a lone pebble that's buried in the weeds of wherever Sophie set us down.

The lights of this Kent remain dark. The city stretches below us, and I can just make out the faint glimmer of bots moving to and fro in the weak, early morning light.

Tools.

Tiff's face scrunches pensively. "And my brother? And Archer?"

Pax's face flames. "I dropped them." His voice is low.

She nods quickly. "I haven't had a minute to ask. I was just freaking grateful they weren't here for this mess, too. Besides, Bry would want to play hero and get his ass beat, as usual."

Jonesy snickers.

That Weller kid *does* like to use his face like a battering ram. Every time.

Tiff glares at Jones. "Shut it, Jonesy."

"Ah, come on, Tiff. Your brother's the tank, baby. If he was here, he'd be taking the most damage for the cause. Ya know it."

Her inhale warbles. "I know." She raises her face to the sunlight. "And I don't *want* him here. But him and Archer *not* being here? *Where* are they?"

"Typically, in a drop, Pax would leave people where the *blink* originated from," John announces.

Hmmm. A memory of getting dropped from an airplane over the Gulf surfaces. I let the thought go. Little too macabre.

"Oh my God, they're in Sanction Police custody?" Sophie asks, looking between Pax and Tiff.

Probably.

"Not for certain. I mean, *they're* not the ones who brought zombies from a parallel plane." Deedie tries for that small hope.

Clyde grunts.

All heads turn. He can't talk anymore. Mouth has gone too soft.

"Clyde," Caleb says in a voice shut down to a single syllable of regret.

Clyde raises his arm, closing the soft fingers of his hand, and a squishing sound erupts from the gesture.

We all wince.

"He's too far gone. Sure, Caleb can repair Clyde when we return home, but with *blinking*, I don't know if degrading mass is reshaped if it's not one hundred percent living tissue. We're taking chances, Caleb," Jeff states.

Caleb cups his chin, mental wheels spinning. "Pax?"

"I can get everyone back, but we're just falling into the SP's laps."

Caleb drops his hand, shaking his head once. "Doesn't matter. We'll have to take our chances back home."

A trick of light causes Jeffrey's eyes to appear almost green, though I know they are a perfect combination of green and brown, and he picks up the thread of conversation where Caleb left off. "If the Thompsons get their hands on me, they'll torture me into naming every human being for the rest of my natural life. No paranormal will be safe. And it's only a matter of time before the Zondoraes of this world perfect regeneration into a virtual fountain of youth like they have on our earth. My future immortality would be ruled by marking paranormals."

Sophie's eyes are wide. "Let's take our chances." Tears stream down her face.

And Tiff's.

Deedie and Jade are tear-free. But Jade's had children, and Deedie's probably too young to understand the loss of what she's never had. Zero point of reference.

Kim doesn't cry because kids aren't revered in this world. On her earth, they keep only the infants who might be of use later, while killing everyone else.

I nod, standing next to Pax. I take his hand. He squeezes it. Not like a sissy. But like an agreement between men.

Men don't always need to speak, to be heard.

A familiar heat flares. Then stops.

"Shit," Pax says, with real fear threading through his voice.

I jerk my head in his direction, lasering my stare at him. "What?" We've worked up to this point, to face the danger we know rather than let Thompson and crew get their grubby hands on our family and friends. *Now what?*

"It's daytime."

Dread floods through me. *Right.* Pax can't *blink* during the day. The second eyelid is ruined by natural light—doesn't even like artificial light much.

A whistling sound zooms pass me as the first dart hits Pax's shoulder, and I jump in my skin. I duck, throwing my hands above my head. "What in the blue blazes!"

Jeff's sharp eyes turn to mine like a startled hawk. "Fuck me," he breathes.

Yessiree.

Darts like arrows arc above us, honing in on us like heat-seeking missiles.

Mitch encircles Deedie with his strong arms, and my great-granddaughter clenches her eyes shut. "*I can try,*" Mitch volunteers, though I don't think anyone but Deedie and I hear him.

Pax staggers toward Deedie, grabs Mitch's arms, and begins to slide down his body, grabbing at his jeans like the side of a boat while drowning. "Tranq," he manages to whisper.

"Shit," Mitch says, easily holding Pax up with one hand.

More darts fall, sinking into our group.

That coward Brad. A stinger glances off the top of my ear, and I rush to grab Pax.

Everyone begins falling like dominoes around us.

"*Blink*, Mitch," Pax whispers, dried saliva gathering at the corners of his mouth, eyelids hooding.

Mitch shifts, moving his back into the line of fire, and five more darts twang into his broad back. His grin spreads, and I know the expression for what it is.

The tranquilizers won't work on him. My gaze sweeps over the gang.

Clyde meets my eyes, and I see the darts sink into the mess of his body then fall out without purchase.

He knows, too.

Our pair of zombies are the last hope.

"It's daytime," Mitch says with a franticness that's not his norm as Brad Thompson stomps toward us with our end in his gaze.

Bots and the dead of this world converge around everyone.

"Do it," Pax says, then slumps into unconsciousness.

Mitch wraps my great-grandson's wrist in the unforgiving hold of the undead.

His second eyelid descends, immediately beginning to smolder on top of his glacial-blue eyeball.

Deedie mewls like a tortured kitten, and I take my hand from Pax and grab ahold of her shoulder.

My gaze travels our fading group, and everyone's linked together like a barrel of monkeys.

Jonesy's got his arm stiff above him with his middle finger extended.

That drops as he loses consciousness. Gotta love his grit.

Mitch *blinks.* God love him. He's a zombie and doesn't feel pain—so he *blinks* us the hell out of this place.

Brad's image wavers like looking through rushing water, along with the open-mouthed screaming bots and fleshy zombie team.

The smell of rot and decay blur, the sound of the mechanical sirens quiet.

The edges of this world are erased, like something seen through a glass, darkly.

23

Deegan

I breathe deeply. Again. Let it out.

And smell. Exhaust (like Gramps's garage).

Refuse.

Humanity.

My eyelids flutter apart, and I feel strong arms bind me to a muscular body. I move to sit up, and those arms tighten around me.

"Mitchell," I say.

"Hmm," he says against my temple. I smell death and the life I gave him swell, and it eases me.

"Mitchell," I say more urgently, my eyes beginning to take in our surroundings. *I don't recognize anything.*

There are no bots, and that should make me relieved. I do know I'm sitting in the middle of a heavily treed neighborhood in my hometown of Kent, Washington. I recognize it.

There should also be relief in that realization.

But the cars cruising past at about thirty miles per hour *on the ground* have my full, terrified attention.

Again, I'm reminded that I loved history before I graduated high school just a month ago. I don't have *any* memory of fossil fuel and only recognize its scent because of Gramps's ancient car, but its not seen mainstream use in at least two decades. There is no point of reference for me.

But I'll just hazard a guess, as Dad would say.

Somehow, Mitch *blinked*. So that means that somewhere in my makeup, I can also *blink*.

And he didn't *blink* to a *where*. He *blinked* to a *when*.

Mitch stands, pulling me up with him. "What in the hell is this?" his voice is quiet. Tight.

I turn my attention in the direction he's looking.

Antique cars begin to slow, clearly noticing a bunch of people rolling around on cement sidewalks.

Gramps hops to his feet, looking more spry than a guy that old should look. But his regeneration continues, and I can tell by the expression on his face that he knows *when* we are. His features go from neutral to troubled in a flash.

Everyone is waking up from the shock of landing, and the cars that drive by hold curious drivers and passengers, checking out the dozen people lying on a sidewalk of what appears to be a quiet neighborhood at— *what time is it?* I look to the sky and notice the sun is low in a distant horizon. Sunset is a promise.

Twilight is near.

Pax will be able to *blink* us out of here. I'm so relieved by the thought that Pax can fix us from *here* that I don't think about why we ended up in this time. Or *how.*

Pax doesn't *blink* us to a timeline other than the one we live in. The present.

"That's my house. I mean, my folks' house." Mitchell's disbelief rides his voice.

What?

Suddenly, a big guy exits the house we're looking at and strides to a souped-up, old-fashioned-looking hot rod.

"Nice car," Gramps says, rocking back on his heels.

The hell with the car. I can't take my eyes off the dude that's about ready to get behind the wheel.

Oh God.

A slightly younger Mitchell stabs a key into the car door then jerks the handle and pops inside. His hands are busy now with stuff like inserting a key into an old-fashioned ignition, adjusting the wheel, and general tasks of starting an old-style car.

I gape at the scene.

"Let's make ourselves scarce," Gramps says in his puzzling way, and we all move silently backward into a small greenbelt, congregating together and thanking everything holy that the Mitchell of now didn't notice all of us conspicuously loitering a block from his house.

As though Mitchell heard our thoughts, he says softly, "I was distracted."

I turn to look at him. He avoids looking at me.

"Why?" I search his face, but my eyes are pulled in the direction of the other Mitchell as his car zooms past. The low purr of the gas-guzzling auto momentarily destroys all potential conversation.

He takes a breath like he's starving for air. "Because I was trying to remember what everyone wanted on their pizza, Deegan." His voice is bald, empty like a scooped out husk.

Oh my God.

Everyone stares at Mitchell.

"This is the day you murdered those men?" Dad asks from across the small copse of trees. His voice carries perfectly. The onlookers are long gone.

Mitchell nods. "It's 2010. I don't know how…" His hands fist.

"Because as a zombie, you'll remember the most traumatic event in your life," Dad says with irrefutable logic.

"Caleb," Mom says, putting her hand on Dad's arm.

"It's true. It's the way the dead work. How they process. We know more now than when I was a kid, and road kill would follow me around. There's a purpose to their thoughts."

Being burnt alive by enemies in a foreign country wasn't the biggest. That wasn't the *most* traumatic thing for Mitchell.

No. Not being here to protect his sister and brother was the most traumatic event.

"I can stop this." Mitchell's eyes become fervent. Hostile. The same eyes I imagine he had when he became a murderer on this day.

"How is this fucking possible?" Pax asks. "I never *blink* to another time. I didn't even know it was possible."

"He unconsciously *blinked* to the *when* that he felt was the most critical juncture when he lived, I surmise," Uncle John says thoughtfully.

Mitchell isn't listening, and I feel his mental withdrawal from me. "I don't have much time. They were watching the house. They're probably already in there."

Mitchell's arms fall from around me, and he begins to walk away.

I don't say anything. *I can't.* Tears tremble at my jawline. Drip, drip, dripping, they soak the fabric of my T-shirt along my collarbone. Cupping my elbows, I bite my lip to keep from crying out.

If Mitchell saves his family right now in this second chance of destiny, the events of the rest of his life will be reordered. That's the way fate operates.

He will not die.

I might not live.

We will not be *more.*

Mitchell suddenly stops.

He turns.

I see by his expression he understands that when bot world happens, Brad Thompson will have me.

Hurt me.

If Mitchell doesn't go to that house where he was raised from a toddler to the young man that I realize I love, he's condemning his family to death.

Pax's hand lands on my shoulder—and passes through.

Oh my God!

I slowly raise my hand and flutter my fingers. I see Mitchell through flesh that was solid a moment before.

My life hangs in the balance of a choice from a man I raised in a moment of terror so great I couldn't think. So I didn't. My ability thought for me, saving me then.

It can't save me now.

Mom screams, and I feel bodies move toward me as though if they're close enough, they can keep me in the present.

"Deegan!" Mitchell bellows. He runs to me. Then sprints.

As his family dies just meters away, I become solid again.

He wraps his arms around me.

"I can't lose you."

His huge body trembles, dwarfing me.

And I can't kill them.

I take his hand and open it. I place my lips in the center of his palm. "Let's go together. Maybe that will be enough."

Jonesy walks up to where we stand. "Don't know what's happening here, guys, but let's get hot. I'm on board for ass-kicking if that's what's on the table." He waggles his eyebrows.

The rest of the group files around us. They don't know the details, but they know enough.

I see the willingness in their eyes. My parents can't stand by while two kids are assaulted and murdered.

Gramps is already on his way to Mitchell's house, Kim's hand in his own.

A tremulous smile curls the corners of my mouth.

I'd rather do one really right thing in my life and die than do a million wrong things and live.

Glass clanks, and a muffled scream reaches my ears.

Mitchell runs toward his childhood home, and I'm tucked against him.

Solid.

For now.

THE END

Watch for **DEATH INCARNATE**, book 9, *coming in 2017!*

If you enjoyed **DEATH BLINKS**, please consider posting your thoughts at your point of purchase and help another reader discover a new series. Thank you!

***Please read on for a sample chapter of another Tamara Rose Blodgett work that takes place in the Death world....

VAMPIRE

An Alpha Claim Brief-Bites® Novelette
Episode 1

New York Times Bestselling Author(s)

MARATA EROS

TAMARA ROSE BLODGETT

1

Narah

My legs are kicked up on the desk, the toes of my left combat boot stacked on the heel of my right. I lean my feet a couple of inches to the left and look at my boss.

Kinda wish I hadn't.

The tongue-lashing was going to be brutal, and not the fun kind. I just barely hold back a snort of self-serving comedy.

"Narah," Casper leans into the desk, edging a butt cheek on the only part not covered by my assortment of shit. My eyebrow cocks. Perturbed doesn't cover it. If I wanted a butt on my desk, I'd ask.

"What?" I bark with anticipation.

A vein in Casper's forehead throbs and I dial it back some. No need to bring the guy to heart failure.

"What?" I repeat more good-naturedly, though both of us know I'm nothing of the sort.

He sighs, scrubbing a palm over his face. Hair almost as white as swan feathers glows under the LED lighting in my tiny office, and his glacial eyes tighten, fighting for a view of my face over the top of my boot.

I jack my feet down and stuff them underneath my desk. My fingers itch to go to my smart phone. Anything to not commit to this conversation.

"You know we appreciate your skill set."

Blah, blah, stinking-blah.

"But we can't have you pulling firearms on all your bounties."

My bottom lip pops out in a pout. "It was a very small gun, Casper." I put my index and thumb almost touching.

"Using manstopper ammunition?"

He might have a small point.

"Outlawed in 1898," Casper adds.

I shrug a bare shoulder, my tank top skin-tight against my small frame. I find loose clothes are handles to make a bludgeon against me easier. I nail the targets but if there's nothing for them to grab onto, so much the better.

"I like antique weaponry and ammunition," I say with deliberate nonchalance.

"Really?" Casper says and I wince at the sound of his voice. "Let's run down the list of target fatalities."

Hmmm.

"Target 103, lethal stabbing."

I lean back in my chair and cock my neck back, staring at the dingy ceiling. A water stain has spread out from the center in a pattern of copper lines that somehow resemble a flower opening.

It's sort of like watching clouds outside, but inside.

"Narah!"

I sigh, answering the ceiling. "Yeah."

"Target 424, beheading."

Yeah, that'd been messy.

"Again, I was in fear for my life," I say, not sounding defensive.

At. All.

"Thirteen times?" Casper asks softly.

My chin snaps down and I meet his eyes. Mine are big and golden hazel like a cat's, and that's why I hide them behind my aviator shades. The sun hurts like hell. I've always been sensitive to sunlight.

I shrug. It'll get me nowhere to fight with Casper. Who has the nickname in the office of, The Ghost. No one says it to his face though. I fight a snicker.

"We are the last profession for use of lethal force, you know. It's not goddamned 2015, when everyone thought all physical force was necessary in some capacity."

I'm in the wrong era, I muse with regret.

"We are the last stand against the criminals of our time. When the police can't nail them, then it's up to us.

But Narah," Casper scrubs his head, his crewcut bristling from the contact, "we can't have you killing all the targets. They must be brought to justice."

And of course, if I kill a target, Casper doesn't get credits. That's what this is *really* about. I bring in the most targets in our office. I get results and he gets credits for my hard work.

We stare at each other. I won't break and Casper knows it. "You're the finest bounty hunter we have. Your instincts are uncanny, and you never let being a woman get in your way..."

I lunge to my feet and Casper jerks to his, eyeing me warily.

Good, my desk is finally free of his ass.

"Nothing about me being a woman comes into play here."

Casper shoots out an exhale like a cannon. "Everything about it matters. You're smaller, you're vulnerable to things a man could never be."

Rape is the clear inference.

"You think a man can't be raped?" I bark out a laugh. "You think that my looks don't disarm. They do, Cas." My eyes laser down on him and his shift away. "You know I'm a proficient, Level Ten."

"Nothing to sneeze at," he concedes and opens his mouth to add more, perhaps dig his grave a little deeper.

I raise my palm. *Nothing to sneeze at.* I can feel a royal conniption fit brewing. "No. If I've killed while gunning for a target," Casper frowns at my wording which causes me to grin, "then they needed dying. Period."

Casper walks to my office door. "I'm sorry, Narah, I've done what I could, but the law states that there can't be more than ten sanctions in one quarter. You have thirteen. I got the bonus three waived." He whips his palm in the air like he's performing a magic trick. "Now you'll have to go before the magistrate."

Fuck. They'd plug me a second ass after a first class reaming. If—*if* I could even bounty again.

I jerk my leather jacket off the back of my chair and sling it on. A bright headache, a new friend of mine of late, settles into my temples with zeal. I press my fingers against my head.

I hate not having a target. The chase is the one thing that makes my life worth living. No longer an outcast—always in the game.

Now the rules are being threatened.

And all I want to do is play.

2

Aeslin

Edan jerks a thumb my way, throwing a towel I deftly catch. I dab at the sweat running like a river from my scalp and making its way to the waistband of my work out gear.

"Corcoran's asking for you."

I look at him, narrowing my eyes.

"Hey man, don't kill the messenger," Edan's hands spread away from his body.

He'd look so much more innocent if he had even one spot of bare skin. Edan's tatted from head to toe. Well... that's not entirely accurate. Don't think his feet hold the tats of our species. Or his face.

Turners are required to be marked.

It's grounds for immediate execution to civilian vampires if they touch us. After all, we're the only savior of our dying race. They can't miss our marks. In the human world, tattoos no longer stand out. We hide in plain sight now.

I flick irritated eyes to him. "I'm on leave, Edan."

He shrugs. "You know the drill. If a female comes on the radar, we're all on alert."

I throw the damp towel in the soiled laundry hamper. I'm bone tired. Not physically—mentally. So many scouting expeditions and coming up empty handed has taken its toll. I rub a hand on my nape, trying to make a raw spot. "I've worked a solid quarter—nothing."

My eyes meet his. Edan's looks are unusual for a Turner. Most of the sub-sect of vampire Turners possess dark coloring. Our only unified feature are silver eyes. Edan's are amber. Some kind of genetic throw back. My own hair is a deep chestnut, more red than what is considered fashionable. And if we want to enjoy female vampire company, it matters. They're few and far between. If they can't be our mates, it's only for release. And that's become an empty vessel.

"But what if we have a live one?"

I smirk at his words. "You mean undead, right?"

Edan throws up his hands. He's muscled, like the rest of us. Mandatory training makes our bodies at battle readiness. Last month we'd just missed a female by minutes.

She'd been sterilized. Technically, it'd been on our watch.

The loss had brought the entire team down and morale had not recovered.

Edan spoke my thoughts, "We need this, Aeslin. We need a female. They're so vulnerable to the Hunters..."

I toss my palm up. "We've been over this. It's a race against them. And they got to that female first." I see guilt on his face and know mine looks the same.

"Then why can't you see that every lead should be followed?"

Tired of fucking losing, that's why. Or just tired.

My eyes feel like they're on fire when I glare at Edan, a Turner I've fought shoulder to shoulder beside. "You don't think it haunts my fucking every thought that she could have belonged to one of us?"

"Does it?" Edan asks in soft disbelief.

"Yes," I hiss defensively.

"Then join us."

I don't want another dead end. Another disappointment. "I'm not rested."

"So when has that ever mattered?" he asks.

Since that female was lost, I think but don't say.

❧

Corcoran stands at the window when I walk into his office and shut the door.

He doesn't turn.

Corcoran is a Noble.

A politically correct word for being in charge of the Turners. But he became a Noble the hard way, having been a Turner first and struggling through the ranks to prove himself invaluable to the cause. Now he rules over the Turners of our region with an iron fist.

Hell, in his day, there was a female turned every month. Now we were lucky to turn one a quarter. However, there was one biological advantage. A human female with vampire blood once turned, was always meant for her biological other half. Lucky bastard. It meant offspring.

A chance at happiness.

With Hunters killing off every vampire they could, our numbers continued to dwindle. In the last half-century, one in two females who possessed enough of the blood of our kind had been sterilized before they could be turned, negating their vampire ancestry and the ability to have children.

A Turners' goals were two-fold. Find the hybrid vampire females before the Hunters did, and determine how they were setting their sights on the rare females.

Easier said than done.

"Aeslin," Corcoran said as greeting.

I remain silent.

Corcoran turns, eyeing me up. "You look rested." He sounds hopeful. We both know I've had only four days respite.

I need a month.

I haven't taken enough blood, had enough sex, slept inside the ground as I should. A lot of *have nots* on the short list of my exhaustion.

I lift my shoulders in an answer that isn't one. It will do no good to rehash the discussion I had with Edan.

Corcoran says something under his breath. It sounds suspiciously like a curse.

"You're the best I have, Aeslin," he says quietly.

"Let Edan take it. Hell—Jaryn could…"

His gaze darkens. Eyes not the common light gray of the Turner are pewter in a face devoid of emotions. Corcoran's gaze is a coming storm.

"I need you on this."

That's just what Edan said. "I mean no disrespect…"

"Yes, you do," he says with the barest bit of humor.

My lips thin. "Yes."

"She's a Turn, Aeslin. I know it." Corcoran closes his fingers into a fist.

My breath leaks out of me in defeat. "Okay."

I simply don't believe anymore. There's been so many dry runs I can't remember the last one that wasn't.

"She's sending out pheromones like a distress signal."

"Who called it?"

His face closes down. "Torin."

Corcoran and Torin don't see eye-to-eye. I say nothing, waiting. I'm not political and won't immerse myself in it now.

Corcoran slams a fist against the wall that bisects the bulletproof windows. "She's bounty."

His frustration gets my attention. Hell, her occupation stalls me and I unlace my fingers and straighten my posture. "What?"

"Damn," he grits through his teeth, knowing fullwell the risks of this acquisition.

I tell him anyway. "Too high profile," I state, hands going to my hips.

"She's manifesting."

Dammit.

"Is Torin sure she's a Turn?"

Corcoran exhales in a rush, taking a rough palm down his face, nodding.

I suck in a deep breath. "I'll do it."

Corcoran looks relieved. "You know the risk?"

Hell yes. But another sterilized female? That we don't need. Can't stand.

"Yes," I answer.

If Torin's got a bead on her, then so do the Hunters.

The thought of a female out there and vulnerable tightens my guts. This is the part of my job I hate. However small, the emotion is there in my suppressed emotional makeup. The hardest to squelch, the most damning.

Hope.

ACKNOWLEDGMENTS

It's been since March 31, 2011, when my first book, *Death Whispers,* was published. I'd like to take this opportunity to thank each and every one of my readers. Without you, I would not have an audience for my work. Your support, recommendations, encouragement, and critical feedback have allowed my improvement as a writer and as a human being. Ironically, words are inadequate for expressing the depth of my gratitude. Please know how much your support has meant and will continue to mean in the future.

Thank you from the bottom of my heart.
Tamara

Dear Ones:
Danny
Cameren*:* Without you, there would be no books.

Thank you:
My Readers
Special thanks *to the following: Beth Dean Hoover, Dii and Shana for all your help and support.*

ABOUT THE AUTHOR

www.TamaraRoseBlodgett.com

Tamara Rose Blodgett: happily married mother of four sons. Dark fiction writer. Reader. Gardner. Dreamer. Home restoration slave. Coffee addict. Digs music.

She is also the *New York Times* Bestselling author of *A Terrible Love*, written under the pen name, Marata Eros, and over eighty-five other titles, to include the #1 international bestselling erotic Interracial/African-American TOKEN serial and her #1 bestselling Amazon Dark Fantasy novel, *Death Whispers*. Tamara writes a variety of dark fiction in the genres of erotica, fantasy, horror, romance, sci-fi and suspense. She lives in the midwest with her family and three, disrespectful dogs.

CONNECT WITH TAMARA

TRB News:
http://tinyurl.com/TRBNewReleaseAlert

BLOG:
www.TamaraRoseBlodgett.com

FaceBook:
http://tinyurl.com/TamaraRoseBlodgettFB

Twitter**:**
https://twitter.com/TRoseBlodgett

Subscribe to my **YouTube** Channel:

http://tinyurl.com/TRBYouTube

Excerpts!
Comedic Quips
Win **FREE** stuff!

CPSIA information can be obtained
at www.ICGtesting.com
Printed in the USA
LVOW10s1658190217
524747LV00001B/27/P